HUMANS

OF FAITH

The nectar of life is the faith within

Humans of Faith
Edited by Arshia Aslam
Print Edition

First Published in India in 2020
Inkfeathers Publishing
New Delhi 110095

Copyright © Inkfeathers Publishing, 2020
Cover Design © 2020 Inkfeathers Publishing
Cover Image © Pikisuperstar from Freepik.com

www.inkfeathers.com

HUMANS OF FAITH

The nectar of life is the faith within

Edited & Compiled by

Arshia Aslam

Inkfeathers Publishing

DISCLAIMER

The anthology "Humans of Faith" is a collection of stories and poems by 32 authors who belong to different parts of the globe. The anthology editor and the publisher have edited the content provided by the co-authors to enhance the experience for readers and make it free of plagiarism as much as possible. All the stories and poems published in this anthology are a work of fiction. Unless otherwise indicated, all the names, characters, objects, businesses, places, events, incidents- whether physical/non-physical, real/unreal, tangible/intangible in whatsoever description used in this book are either the product of the author's imagination or used in a fictitious manner. Any resemblance to actual persons, objects, entities, living or dead, or actual events is purely coincidental. The stories and poems published in this book are solely owned by their respective authors and are no way intended to hurt anyone's religious, political, spiritual, brand, personal or fanatic beliefs and/or faith, whatsoever.

In case, any sort of plagiarism is detected in the stories and poems within this anthology or in case of any complaints or grievances or objections, neither the anthology editor, nor the publisher are to be held responsible for any such claims. The author(s) who holds the rights to the particular story or poem, shall be held responsible, whatsoever.

CO-AUTHORED BY

Abul Hasan Ali ~ Matthew Gibney ~ Diksha Raman ~ Myra Lake ~
Sistla Shravya ~ Bhavya Jain ~ Rachith Reddy ~ Duni Porter ~
Insanely Nerd ~ W.P.T Moreno ~ Madiha Shamsi ~ S.M. Tucker ~
Sarah Kesteven ~ Aditya Mandhania ~ Sheryl Lazer ~ Morgan
Makowski ~ Ranjit K. ~ JD Maxwell ~ Joshua Prince ~ Sulagna
Samanta ~ Jagruthi Kommuri ~ Shomama Islam ~ Dr. Apteena
Johnson Kakkadu ~ Rebecca Nelson ~ Shivani Sharma ~ Isidora
Radovanac ~ Sam Julio Fortes Neves ~ Manoj Vaz ~ Kaitlyn Leiva ~
Divyansh Dwivedi ~ Rosanna Purkiss ~ Jennifer Gellock

CONTENTS

Poetry

Story

ABOUT THE EDITOR

ARSHIA ASLAM

Being 'natural and yourself' has been her goal since forever. Arshia is a sweet, fun, romantic and elegant mare with a peaceful heart. Basically, a half-human, half-weaponized automaton dead set against hackneyed ideas of humanity. She focuses on the next ceiling she can break, the next big thing she wants to achieve, rather than wasting her time fighting with people and worrying about them. Being blessed with myopia, her eyes like things close up: lovers, babies, cheese toasts, flowers, raindrops.

Arshia Aslam experimented with various sidelines but what began as a grad school hobby is now her favorite escape - not going a day without writing. As an author or co-author, she has published four anthologies. 'The Abode of Poems' is her debut book. As a web content writer, she has written for NGOs and ecommerce sites. Besides, she has gathered numerous accolades in open mics and orations.

She enjoys caffeine, as should all right thinking people. Her write-ups are strong and fearless, but in real life, Arshia is afraid of elevators, dogs, and going up stairs when it is dark behind her. When she isn't reading or writing romantic verses, Arshia is probably painting, watching The Fault in Our Stars with an ice cream bowl, or dreaming of Ian Somerhalder. Frivolous coffee dates, stargazing and going for midnight walks and drives are the things that interest her. Her other talents include prolific cursing, spilling/dropping things, accidentally making people awkward and dancing.

As a writer, Arshia tends to see intricacy in the uneventful moments of life that makes her stop, stare and ponder. She likes to represent these whiffs of life to her readers, with a spin, so that they too can appreciate the beauty in all things simple. She hopes to foster a sense of self-awareness and confidence through her profession, just as she seeks to do through her passion.

All she wants in her life is '*To Love and Being Loved*'.

EDITOR'S NOTE

I believe in God, but not as one thing, not as a childish man in the woods. I believe that what people call God is something in all of us. A belief that confirms that the universe is aligned, that the world's greatest resource is love, and maybe even that God is one.

I've been writing for quite long. Since the day I started penning down my emotions I always wished to let this thing grow more, get fierce, like an electric current in my veins, my blood type and you see, here I am presenting before you my first ever book as an editor. I got my poems published for the very first time in an anthology, titled 'The Abode of Poems' which was compiled by Tanishk Singh, an amazing human being. The book is by far the greatest thing that ever happened to me in 18 years of my life. And too that it was published under Inkfeathers Publishing, I became a part of this family since then. I used to stay connected with them, and the day when I got to know that they're recruiting editors, I didn't find a single reason to let go of this opportunity!

We had the freedom to choose a particular theme for our anthology, and the one I chose is the closest to my heart. It's a compilation based on spirituality, divinity of God, ideologies of faith, faith tales and struggles in finding faith.

I believe I was never born spiritual, neither do any other human being on this planet. It's just that how certain experiences and aspects of life brings us tawakkul (God's consciousness). And when I gained reliance on Him alone, I wanted it to be recognized by my fellow human beings too, instead of just discussed as a theoretical concept. I wanted to plant this conviction in their hearts, and what could be better than poetry and story scripting in gravitating them towards trusting this virtue.

Talking about the book that I'm going to present before you, is a garland to the light and dark literatures equally. The finest compilation of amateurish phrases and gloomy realities. Where at some point you'll find a test of inner strength, next will take you to numinous otherworldly visions and everything is undoubtedly expected, after all it's a theme based collection, in here you'll get to know that there's a supreme but incorporeal being called God, the dogmas of faith, the rings of scars and struggles, and ultimately a total submission to God!

I'd only say that my first book as an editor, rather our book is already the greatest success to me so far. I'm so spellbound by all of the co-authors included from different regions of the world map. I tried to dedicate each and every atom of my body and poured my blood, sweat and tears into this treasury. I thoroughly enjoyed working on this project and I'll always remember this experience.

I hope that it'd be a worth reading compilation for the readers.

Enjoy the essence!

Arshia Aslam,
Editor

POETRY

FAITH- INQUISITIVE RESETTLEMENT

Abul Hasan Ali

By dwindling flares
Of light on the railing
And anxious flutters
Of every caged avian
To fates undeciphered
And hopes forsaken
Of arches skeletal
And foundations crumbling
Questions, dealt and dodged
With words less and frowns more
Unlike quarrels, by the counter side
Parried by the pact of bond, a contract
Carried by neither, ignorant divide
Persists in the veins, a deterrent impact

Merely a permiss, sandwiched by
Pain and forbid, a chance to speak
Relief to act, scriptural references
Must not you seek?

Justice, of moral inclinations
Of independent petitions
Of unbreached isolation
From One and His command
And His message to convey
Steadfast and never to sway
For mortal years mimic sand
Intimate to believers the core of creed
Of belief, rattled and resettled, by men freed
And disillusioned, toiling to unswathe,
The chosen Humans of Faith.

2

ANIMALIA

Matthew Gibney

A drop of smoking coffee dribbled slowly down my thigh,
that cliff, soft, white as death, of which I've come to love so dear.

Black on pale cream and so I suffocate a cry,
without a fleeting thought I raise a paw to sweep it clear, then drop it
with a thud upon a nicotine stained desk.

Where ink and sweat and tears and I turn iron into gold,
and pause to ask a question with which we alone are blessed.

Why oh why in heaven should I render fire cold?
What lack of cerebellum makes us wish to follow this?

This blasted, hissing urge, that nerves so sharp beg us to heed,
Yes, we, with brains of gold and light waste lives in search of bliss,

Weep and gnash and claw and wail every time we bleed.
Us kings of animals who carry "rich, immortal souls"
Us who your fabricated master chose to be his own,

So, tell me how the "worthy" lords of iron, fire, and coal,
still scream unholy agonies when shrapnel scratches bone?

If life on earth is but a bittersweet aperitif,
and bliss begins when the blood stops coursing through my heart.

If I should choose to live within your crumbling belief
then tell me what it is that sets us and the beasts apart?

3

MY UNSEEN GUIDE

Diksha Raman

Every pain, every journey, every fall, and every win has something to
convey, something to relish and teach.
Doesn't it feel like we always have someone supporting our back,
providing us with unseen strength?

When we sink and drown, when they just laugh
looking at our defeated face,
isn't there something divine that keeps us motivated to keep running
in the lifelong race?

Seeing often leaves things left to be noticed, but feelings never hide.
Such faith I carry within myself, when I surmise about the creator, my
unseen guide.

Unseen and untouched, but I always felt that divine being around me
as my protective shield.
Whenever I wanted to give up, it stopped me and took my mind and
soul miles away to break and rebuild.

No arms, no ammunitions, the divine being perhaps possesses some magical stick.
When things are messed up, it clears up everything just at a blink.

I feel despaired, I cry out, I scream in front of those crafted bodies and heads.
At the end, my heart feels light as a feather, as if someone took all my woe and relieved me in its shade.

When all obstinate turns up and I feel lost and sick.
That power from within screams as if I am not meant to break down so quick.

It is easy for them to say, that divine being doesn't exist.
It feels toilsome for me to march forward without its benediction and blessings.
My faith on that supernatural being is sinless and unending,

The way it deposits hopes and dreams on my tiny eyes, that passion is never ever fading.

4

SEEKING GOD

Myra Lake

Some people look for God
Within the walls of a church.
But I've had better luck
In the shade of a towering birch.

I feel my God in the flowing waters,
And hear Him speaking through knotty pine,
But I've never looked to a building
When I sought a symbol or sign.

Such a beautiful world He created for us,
Everything we ever would need.
Plants and creatures he put in our midst,
That we might shelter, heal, and feed.

Yet so many turn their back on His work,
Saying it's savage and raw.
They spend their lives trying to escape
And ignore His natural law.

The more I open my eyes and heart
To the wonder of His creation,
The more I find myself overjoyed
In awe and pure elation.

I read more of God's love in the song of a bird
Than I have in any book,
And I find more of His teachings every day,
Nearly every place that I look.

Nature is not savage,
It is humans who earn that name,
As we destroy it for our own greed,
And refuse to accept the blame.

So when I am seeking God,
I look for a glade or a glen
And find Him in His creation,
Not in the buildings of men.

5

A SUTON

Sistla Shravya

It all begins from a suton.
When you come to realize it, life has taken it's another bend.
So, don't try to amend, just learn to blend.
Never feel ashamed to bend.
He's here to dictate, not to amate.
Why these give ups, can't you take your stand ups?
You're an enigma of your own kind, having quiddity of His.
You're a part and always will.
It all begins from the only end.
So don't stop let them think morosis.
Let them live in habromania,
But you; you have your own eunoia.
Let the end be a start of new; where you and he are no hate.
What a beautiful sweven!

6

ANGER AND LOVE

Bhavya Jain

There was a time,
A time there was love,
Clearly seen between us.
Not like that unseen dove.
By the time we were child,
We had no fights,
Only beautiful flights,
There were no conflicts,
Even ego didn't come in between,
There were no rifts,
Only beautiful embrace,
And grace,
Love was shown face to face,
Not like now,
Like in a race.
Now it's something different,
Ego, rift, conflict
Has taken over us.
We betrayed us.

Like the lion of the jungle,
Behave like a king,
But at the end eat everyone,
Now no one to bow below him,
We lost ourselves,
We lost our relations,
There was a time,
There was a smile.

There was a time,
We didn't argue over a load of things,
Now we search for those
Like a thorn in a pack of straws,
There was a time,
A time
There was love,
Clearly seen between us,
Not like that blurred lines
Or indecipherable writing of an infant.

Anger is the parasite
That lives inside us,
With our knowledge
Yet makes us helpless.

It is like a switch
We never want to turn on,
Manually or automatically,
But
Circumstances make us do that,
Results are beyond the clouds,

Not in our reach,
Unbearable yet beatable,
Anger leaves us,
In the apex,
We in predicament
Making us imbecile,
Disturbing our sanity.

Anger is not courage,
For courage there must be
Something at stake,
For anger we
Throw everything,
Gaining nothing.

Anger is nothing
But our own guilt,
These five letters
Are still unfathomable.
Enough to vanish our existence,
Destroy our resistance.
There was a time,
There was a smile.
Now our own self
Betrayed ourselves.

Anger is left over,
And
Love is over

7

SURFING OVER THE TIDES OF LONESOME

Rachith Reddy

To have people
To go to the restaurants with
And to the movies
But not to talk to
Is difficult.

To have friends
That throw you into the pool
But not those
That pull you out of it
When you tripped
Is disheartening.

When you are invited to every party
But no one misses you
If you haven't shown up
Leaves you feeling
Less than a whole.

I've walked by the beaches alone.
I sat by the window pane alone.
As a sense of inferiority
Started taking root in me
And my self-worth
Became a constant debate.

But in all that time
I've been alone,
Your hand
Has been a steady weight on my shoulder
Always reassuring.

Thank you
For honoring my faith.
It is all that kept me
From drifting into loneliness

8

MY FACE

Duni Porter

I've died a million times this week.
Faces who match mine with their limbs being exploited by blue men
with badges.

It's more than a feeling when a lump in my throat turns to stone as
they reveal my face yet again as someone who has died at the hands of
police brutality.
You'd think they'd be tired of killing me.

No, it's just my face they continuously dismember and claim they
know no better.
Every time I see my face, I wonder who is going to be next.

9

SOLIDARITY

Sistla Shravya

A solitary cloud's rains; are actually tears of pain.
Loneliness was my companion.
I don't know why he forgot to give me lines.
Scars from the past appear like a curse!
I was all alone with the tears to console.
In amidst of struggles, not a single soul cares.
The time I analysed something ultimate,
the tears blurred the stars in dark.
Now when they're having their departure, I can see my future.
A solitary cloud still rains; letting the scars from past drain.

ANXIOUSLY ALIVE

Insanely Nerd

Feeling the darkness invade my soul,
I look around for something to hold.
The walls are closing into my space,
My heart is beating fast like in a race.
The wind is shallow,
Making me gasp for the air.
The land if shifting,
Like it's on a gear.
The sky is burning with the fire,
The moon once silent is no longer quiet.
I remember the God's, the old and the new,
For all sins I did I must repay the dues.
Cannot fathom the lies I told to myself,
Red is flashing across my eyes,
Is this the reality of my life or just a nightmare.
This is the deep slumber I need to survive,
making my soul anxiously alive.

11

FAITH WITHIN

W.P.T Moreno

Lonely darkness
Within and
All around.
Who is there to lead us out?

Frightening storms
Within and
All around.
Who is there to calm it down?

Helpless chaos
Within and
All around.
Who is there to make sense of it?

A distant light illuminating the darkness.
Single rays of sunshine creeping through the sky.
A faint sense of wisdom and purpose.
Who is there?

I take a deep breath.
I face all these feelings.
Loneliness, solitude
Fright, worry
Helplessness, desperation
And see all the strength I need.
Not searching outside,
But finding within.
What a wonderful world
If we had
Believe and faith
In ourselves.

12

BLENDING OF SOUL AND GOD

Madiha Shamsi

I'm a lonely traveler
Waiting for someone to make my confidence grow more.
Exploring through the growing roads.
Across the world of possessions.
I'm somewhere lost in tranquility.
My soul wants to breathe,
But the mind wants to be in the cloudy trees.
Clouds full of hope are moving slowly.
The still breeze is calm.
I'm captivated in the moment.
And my soul is unable to escape
In the startling night,
The light of God reached my soul.
As it touched my wings,
My soul started flying.
In my own world,
In my eyes
I felt like blending with the God is the only option.

13

THE FLYING ANT

SM Tucker

A flying ant was caught in a web and
I thought I might save her for a while,
long live the queen, but my hand suddenly stalled
when I thought that the spider might die.

So I turned and I walked off and left her
to a fate that no monarch should meet,
the silk strings she plucked to each step I took
and I think now I know how God feels.

14

APRICITY IN FELICITY

Sistla Shravya

If everything around is dark look again, maybe you're the light.
You're the apricity in this felicity.
Dear Sofia, I know you want your metanoia, but it's just your hulya.
As for that you need eunoia.
So just listen to yourself.
Dear Sofia, I agree you've your blues.
But let your hurricane be a halcyon.
If everything around is dark look again, maybe you're the light.
As my Sofia, everyone here is a meraki.
I think now you understood that the forelsket wasn't because of him but of you.
You're not just a sweven, you're his only seven.
 You're the apricity in this felicity.

15

I WAS AN ATHEIST

Sarah Kesteven

No one told me I could believe in God too.
I thought that was something everyone else got to do.
The church goers and girls with scarves,
The old people, dumb people, those with dark hearts.
See my family told me science was key.
It explained it all, easy as one two three.
So I was alone.
In the night I was alone,
When I cried I was alone,
When we were sat round the table with all the love in our hearts,
I couldn't express it while still sounding smart,
But of course, there was something.
Otherwise I don't want to be here,
A Godless, heartless, loveless world.
Where sex is breeding,
Pleasure is programming,
Beauty is a lie,
Just something you've convinced your eye.
Yes, my smile releases chemicals,

But my choice to do that
Came from somewhere else.
Yes, people die and starve, and lives are ripped apart,
And science explains that by the simplicity of life.
That we have nothing to protect us,
That we have nowhere to go, nothing to do
But survive, and to do that we created this hive
Of murder, theft, dishonesty, and inequality.
They ignore a God because what God.
But it was not God, in the omnipotent, impotent
Man in the sky lie.
It was nature.
And she is fallible just like us.
She makes mistakes and stuff fucks up.
Cause we are not controlled, merely created.
And we create too.
But when you ask,
When you need,
She will be there,
You will be seen.
There is a power you can witness,
Evidence for my cause,
Because when you truly trust, believe and work
Things will come to you,
In weird ways we get what we want.
And yes, there is suffering,
But within that suffering there is hope, strength, and a power
To create a new, change, even forgive those
Who hurt,
Those who think they're above God.
Kings sending boys to war,

White thinking they're above black,
Men above women.
This comes from misinterpretation,
It is human error.
Error to see that they're just like me,
Equal connection to God
Equal ability to be a fucking sod
Equal right and equal care.
But some people just don't see that,
They think others were put here
For their use.
They see God only in themselves,
They don't see that Allah's power is the same as Christ's,
They don't see that we are all connected to a source,
From man, woman to tree or horse.
They do not respect life like it is a God.
And that is why they hurt
That is what they forgot.

16

HIGHER

Aditya Mandhania

Hey brother take me higher
To a new world of inner peace.
Where pieces do not split as races or creeds.
Or with all creatures except human.
Coz they are the creepy modern demons.
Of course, I'm too not born as a human.
Either Make me an eagle,
Let me fly beyond the sky.
Or an earthworm
To get buried deep down the soil
But away from this toil and moil.
Either make me the feather,
Flying along the wind.
Carelessly I would grind.
I know I gotta too many scars
Fed up of hiding them all.
Just hitting with every fall.
Dreamt of standing too tall
But shit has got me surround.

Tuning with stereotypes haunts me.
Trying to fake, got me drowned.
Wanna heal the deep wounds
And listen to my inner soul sounds.
Curious for the real 'me' to be found,
Just get me higher and fly around.
With no boundaries bound,
Release all my material bond.
In this mean world I wouldn't count,
Now world feels like a scary mythology,
Where who has the time for eco biology?
Time to doubt about own's psychology,
Having evil power 'technology'.
Incapable of utilizing it
Trying to behave as a prodigy.
The world just makes me suffocate.
It's time for people to re-educate.
Hate to ejaculate,
And humanity to re-evaluate.
Love: to heavily circulate.

17

MET A MAN

Sistla Shravya

I met a man once,
taking deep breaths.
The cast of moon shattered his secrets.
He stood still calmed & hypnotized by the scene.
Soon the air picked up the wandering soul.
The night was dark & deepening.
left me shivering while standing.
Beneath my shoe was a crunching pearl,
I leant & picked up the only dream,
Clasped in my hands as I walked away,
thinking why would a man like him left it.

18

I SAW HER

Sarah Kesteven

I saw God.
I saw her in the sunlight ripping through the clouds.
And I heard God,
Yeah I heard her, in that song,
I hadn't heard it since we'd listened to it.
But to hear it again,
Without anyone around.
It was just me,
And every nook and cranny of my existence.
And there was that song.
Being reverberated back to me
with messages.
I understood cause I was trying to look.
And in everything I saw God.
She was listening
And hoping,
And wondering
Just like me.
And when we looked together there was something new to see.

19

THE MIDNIGHT MIRALE

Sheryl Lazer

Reminiscing memories, sipping my way into the past through a cup of coffee.
I travelled back into the abyss of time,
To the days when my soul was brutally shattered into mere fragments of hopelessness and dejection.
It was the fall I was willing to deny.
Triggered venomously by love and trust.
Lost in a world full of unrecognizable faces,
I rebuked myself for not justifying life's purpose enough.
In the mess of broken dreams,
I stood aloof.
If only I could make it through.
Silenced by the quarreling, the still roaring voices inside of my head.
The time was slowly drifting into the clutches of dead end.
In the last attempt to savour my blank canvas.
I sat under the sky, so full of stars,
Desperately searching for clear answers.
For decades, it had hidden stories of adventure, heart breaks and guilt.

Maybe it could hide the scars I carried within, inside its wonderous possibilities of space and limits.

That midnight, I saw a shooting star.

And in it's aura, I experienced the existence of a greater spirit.

Supernatural and content.

Yet, delicate.

A force driving my intentions, I was not afraid of the repercussions.

Today, as I look back,

Nothing makes more sense to me than the defeats, pain, and rage.

Destiny infact, has it's own ways.

20

THE DIVINE INTERVENTION

Rachith Reddy

I stand at an impasse.
As I feel a force,
Drag me down.
Despite my best efforts,
To rise beyond.
A force I couldn't see,
Oh God as I could never see you.

"Why should I believe in something
I've never seen?"
I always questioned.

"Faith is reliance.
An illusion
Masked in transcendence."
I always told myself.
But I now lay strangled by strings.
Unseen by human eye.

For long I have believed
Success shall be the becoming
Of happiness
And peace.

Step after a step,
One cliff after another,
I ventured.
Without ever looking back.
Now I stand at a great height.
But I fail to realize
All that I sought.
All the momentary laughs,
And the illusion of success
Has accounted to nothing.
My heart still beats impatiently,
Looking for something
That can make it feel at peace.

Is peace an illusion too?
Like faith?
But I long to feel it
In every breath
And in every restless action
I take toward greater success,
Relentlessly.

"Help me oh god.
The devil I bred in ignorance
Has me in its clutches."
I plead in despair.

"Let your faith guide you"
A voice spoke.
The voice I chose to ignore
On several occasions previously.

"Your faith is your resolve.
Not subjugation or reliance
But resolve."
A weapon.

21

FATE

Sistla Shravya

Does the sun promise to shine?
No, but it's apricity never fails to reach us.
Does the moon promise to glow?
No, but it shows it's beautiful side;
Hiding its dark, for not having a choice.
The sun sings it's aubade for its moon in saudade,
though the moon be an astrophile.
Have you ever felt this feeling, that thrust you to move forward,
Even when you are done?
Running away from things, jumping high to overcome obstacles,
May give you abstraction but the reaction will never be a satisfaction.
If you ever felt this, then you should have known that it's fate.
It's his fate in you which helps you to.
You can't quit even if you want to,
As God is still not done with you.

22

WHISPERING WINDS

Morgan Makowski

The wind whispers in my ear
telling me secrets that nobody knows
here it comes... I feel as it blows
hair whips across my cheeks
eyes closed without a peek
I hear the wind, but what is it telling me?

under the pines I sit
plunged in stillness and silence
for peace of mind I stay for a bit
I feel the wind, but what does it mean?
deeply submerged in the nature that surrounds me
waiting to find the proverb it provides me.

23

FEELS

Ranjit K.

Empty vessels stacked upon.
Darkest war I wish I had won.
The end is not near.
The life is yet away far away.
Feelings are hard to be worn.
It's just the way I have to be gone.

24

LITTLE ACTS

Sarah Kesteven

You can call it faith or trust or hope,
Or God.
And it will wrap you up,
And let you sleep,
Bring you peace,
And move your feet.
When I was alone and crying out to the darkness.
I finally decided to change the darkness in my mind,
To faith in something I was blind to see,
Something never been taught to me
Never been part of my community.
But I chose to believe
And that brought clarity,
And my kitty
Came running in
Like he was called by a power,
To come and comfort me.
These small acts of god,
Keep you believing,

And while you believe
Magic is created.
Faith is rewarded,
The world can be beautiful,
Karma can right your wrongs
Allah does hear your songs
Your whispered prayers are loud to God's ear,
And there is a reason why we are all here.

25

A BEAUTIFUL

Sistla Shravya

What a beautiful scenario,
hurtling on this planet.
Indulged heads, bulging on their bed.

What a beautiful scenario,
hurtling on this planet.
Shaking hands with one; breaking touch
with another.

What a beautiful scene,
Nothing left to be pretty,
No one knows colorful,
Nobody even cares.

A perfect world; dust a synonym for success, doubt an antonym.
Do what is said being a slogan here.

When will these humans understand that
human development is greater than the economic.

Working for hours doesn't pay, working with hours do.

What happened; in this race we forgot why
we started?

Let's again make this world "what an ugly
scenario."

26

SAVIOR

JD Maxwell

Not long ago out from the sand,
I wandered to the promised land,
And as I spoke I then did see.
That all of them would follow me.

The more I spoke, the people grew,
To see from Earth a different view,
With all I used my gift to heal,
To show them all I am for real.

And as we move to present day,
I still remain to show the way.
Although there is a larger sum,
It's still to me my people come.

They come to me to see the light,
To take away their endless night.
I give them hope that they shall live,
Through wicked sins that I forgive.

They come to me so they can hear,
The ways to take away their fear.
And from all those to whom I speak,
The ones who live shall be the meek.

Through thirsty times they will be fine,
They see the water turn to wine.
But soon enough I shall be gone,
To bring about another dawn.

So put on me a thorny crown,
And let my people wander down.
Let them see the king of men,
To let them know, I'll rise again.

With every day I shall live on,
Past the days that you are gone.

So even when I cannot stand,
The word of God will spread the land.

27

MOON CHILD

Insanely Nerd

The night was going deep
And the thoughts were in sinking steep.
The hour was late
But the surrounding was bait.
I looked at the moon
He looked at me and smiled.
In that weary moment I knew
I was a moon child.

The sky was dark,
The stars were shining.
There was a light in the ark,
Like Heaven's door was opening.
Once again, I looked at the moon
He looked at me and smiled
In that weary moment I knew
I was a moonchild.

I walked into the space,
Looking for a newer pace
The soul was mystified.
Anxiously artistified,
Now again I look at the moon.
He looks at me and smiles.
In this weary moment I know
I am a moonchild.

28

A HEART

Sistla Shravya

With millions of hair, billions of cells,
& trillions of thoughts is accompanied a heart.
Function is mere pumping but can make anyone jumping.
If heart is used properly gives a start, leaving the rats.
You & he were never apart, the whole will come to you.
Draw a heart, starting from one ending at the same point,
if wanna complete.

There comes a dig as a point where you find your one, but in order to
complete you've to love yourself.
A heart's function is mere pumping but can make anyone jumping.
Don't lose yourself to fit.

29

DESPERATE WHYS

Joshua Prince

Lord, are you hearing me?
Are you watching me?
I am falling without getting up,
I want to stand for you,
Walk for you, live for you,
But, all I can do is go far from you.

I heard of you,
The one who can create,
out of nowhere,
whose one word is enough,
to make something new,
to do a great miracle.

Still, It's been too long,
Since I heard any words,
If you could make me good,
Why don't you do it?
Lord, I am frustrated,

At least answer to this,
What all you do is: increasing my pain.
Abba! My father!

I know you are speaking,
I am listening,
I realize that you can do anything,
But, still you gave me the struggle,
But more grace, to win over it.
I am your favorite crafted vessel,
For the lost.
The creation for winning them,
To make them new.
He can do it with His word, without me;
But He loves to fulfil His word through me,
Coz I am His miracle for them.

30

ESCAPING CHAINS

Sulagna Samanta

Abruptly she woke up from her dreams
Where she has been chased by some unseen presence,
Where she has been followed by some unseen gaze.
Abruptly she woke up from her dreams.
Realizing she madly wanted to escape.

She squeezed her brows and
Half opened her eyes
A burning sensation in the skin that forces to die.
She found herself lying on the cold floor
In a corner of a shadowed room.
As she got up, her arms felt the weakness,
Her head felt the heavy ache
And as she tried to raise her palm
She found her wrist that has been chained.
Shocked she was and was more horrified.
She could make no sense of what was going on
And what she needed to decide.
She tried twice and thrice

And many more to get rid of the chains,
With each preceeding struggle
Her hopes seemed to get failed.

She now dared to look around the room,
For a way to escape, soon she realised
it's a known room, a room of a house
which she knows since her childage.
She couldn't see it clear, no colours,
No more tears because it was her place.
She couldn't understand if
The room is colourless
Or it's just the light that couldn't invade.
She then looked at herself, her body, legs, hands and face.
On a cracked mirror that was silently watching her from a distance.
Strange that she couldn't see the colour of her skin, her hairs, eyes and lips.
All that was visible in its pigment
Was the colour of the bruises and blood oozing from her head, nose, arms, and knees
Which suddenly aroused her pain.

Neither she could hear any noise.
Rather the silence started piercing her eardrums,
She squeezed her eyes and groaned in help.
She put her hands to protect her ears,
From the noise that was making her more helpless.

She screamed out loud with all her pain and fear,
And all of a sudden, she could hear the soothing sound of the breeze,
She missed a shoulder where

She wanted to shed tears.
But now she was at little relief,
Because finally she could hear the air,
Which consoled her that she was no longer alone there.

Gathering some courage, she tried
To stand up and she did.
She took six to seven steps, her ankle was pulled, she fell with a leap.
As she fell down on the floor
Against her chest,
She saw a frame that was in pieces and the picture was torn.

The picture had more than three smiles,
The picture left with some love to be defined.
And now that the picture was torn into pieces,
Smiles could no longer be seen on the faces.
She could realize that she was very much in the present
Where she could hear her breath and count them down.
Her breath turned heavy,
She looked back and found her ankle was chained alike her wrist
And she frowned.

Again she dared to look around the room,
For a way to escape, again realized it's a known room,
A room of a house which she knows since her childage.
The broken frame and the room seemed to have no difference.
It had no doors, no ventilation,
But only a window that was sealed with a black glass,
Which was broken in a corner allowing the air to pass.

Soon she realized it was not her bruises and blood that only exposed

their colours,
Brutal so there stood an iron pillar beside her where words were
carved on it.
But later were crossed out with anger
And her chains were firmly attached to the pillar.
She felt warm air pass by her ears and chill through her spine,
As she understood she has been imprisoned by the suffering so each
day and night.

Abruptly she woke up from her dreams realizing she madly wanted
to escape.
Abruptly she woke up from her dreams
Where she has been chased by some unseen presence
Where she has been followed by some unseen gaze.
Abruptly she woke up from her dreams
Where she was imprisoned by her pains
Where her wrist and ankle were all chained.

31

FAITH IS ALL WE NEED

Rachith Reddy

Faith is all we need.

In each of us
There exists a force,
Unforeseen and ethereal.

Its presence ever so real,
Its anonymity its power
And its authenticity absolute.

Give it a name and call it God
Or let your perception
Define it differently.

It guides you just the same.
You doubt it,
You shall doubt yourself,
Your purpose and your resolve.

Acknowledge,
It shall serve you just.
A little faith is all you need.

32

SECOND NATURE

Duni Porter

Don't force your religion down my throat like a half-eaten orange still
wrapped in its skin.

I chew and swallow your prayers that I'll be the good girl with a bible
in her hand and no longer embarrassing you to your church friends.

I've felt the holiness and showered in its presence only to be rejected
by your tolerance.

If God is everywhere
Can he see me reaching my hands out only for them to be slapped
away by His "people."

33

INTIMATE SOUL

Insanely Nerd

The reflection of your sight,
The sound of your mind,
The look of your smile
Makes my heart agile.
The tenderness of your touch
Brings out your core so much.
Caressing your flawless skin I might
Deepen this bond with some ignite.
The lights that hung low
Are now going to deep glow.
Feeling your soul touch mine.
I can't help skipping the rhyme.
The poetry of your frame,
I can recite all its fame,
The story of your life
Is like a novel I get to recite.
All the night spent in haze
The dew grew in the daze.
My deeds must have been right
For I get to call you mine.

34

ONCE UPON A TIME

Sistla Shravya

This world was started with "once upon a time."

Where I made everyone their only prime.
By distributing this status you've created your callous.
The prime was always you, then why this crime?
You started finding me in others while
I was enlightening in you.

By walking in dark you've made yourself a shark.
This soul I gave you; you to realize that
I'm the light shining as bright.
I've faith in you!
I'm the fake in you!
This world started with "once upon a time."
This world will end because of its only kind.

35

CAN YOU HEAR ME

Sarah Kesteven

I found God,
Because I was scared and alone.

I reached out,
When there was no one in my phone,

I could trust.

I went to the precipice of insane,
And almost jumped.
But I tried one thing first.
Maybe if I called to God,

I would be heard.
And I was.

36

EVERYWHERE

Jagruthi Kommuri

In the depths of oceans deep,
As you conceal yourself to weep,
In the darkest caves you hide,
To deal with all of your pride.

In the valley that is shallow,
As you endure the rivers' flow.
At the heights of mountains' top,
When there's no one to stop,

As you try to find yourself,
in places no one's been there,
You find God Himself,
He is with you everywhere.

37

OUT OF MY MIND

Insanely Nerd

Looking at the dawn I tried to smile.
Wasn't it supposed to be a new beginning,
I despised.
Looking at the moon going down on the side,
I knew love was finally out of my mind.

Scars once beautiful now felt like knives.
Past once accepted now felt redefined.
Looking at my reflection in confide,
I knew love was finally out of my mind.

Kindness was the virtue.
This tale was so true.
Feeling the lies,
Once again stopping the truth.
Forbidden to forget,
Terrified to remember.
I looked at the world from a new angle.
Deciding the fate, I had long back denied,
I knew love was finally out of my mind.

38

EVERY BLOCK

Sistla Shravya

Why to pray rock when you're there in every block.

This generation started assuming but you're their glooming.
glooming for the failures of your creation.

This generation, sinful, dreadful, but still hopeful.
All because of you.
The Rock motivates to do , to help.
I as one of them promise that one day your gloom will turn bloom.
Instead of we will become us.
A place where sins are found in dustbins.
Where no girl would be afraid to talk.
Where no child would be afraid to walk.
A place where light will be you shining in us bright.
No rocks will be needed as you'll be there in every block of us.

39

NO CHURCH

Sarah Kesteven

I do not believe in or support any church.
I know they've done some good, but also a lot of hurt.
I'm a rebel in my soul,
So I don't want to be told how to believe.

God's relationship is with me.
I don't want this catholic lie
That god only talks to those up high.
He is with us all.

Even when you think your life is small.
If church helps you
Use it. But do not let it use you.
Do not let it manipulate your faith,
Don't let them teach you hate.

God gave you your own thoughts
Be brave enough to follow them.

40

PRAY WITH A CLEAN HEART

Shomama Islam

Praying is the first solution of every kind of problem.
All the situations and problems that you want to overcome.

There are times when we feel low, heavy, sad, a little bit of insecure
and unconfident
In those touchy times, we need to get close to God and should pray
with full consistent.

When there is no one to listen, when there is no one to talk, no one
with whom our feelings could be shared.
Remember, God is always there to listen, He is always waiting for us
to talk, as He is the only one who truly cares.

When we want to cry out loud, in the hope that someone would
come to wipe our tears.
But we find, there is no one who cares about our tears but God, as
only He can make our wounds clear.

God is always there for us when we lose ourselves
He guide us, He knows us from depth and He always helps us.
Prayer is where our heart finds peace and soul gets relaxed.
God created us and to Him each and everything is attached.

So, when the things aren't going in our way,
We must put our knees down and pray.

Believing in God and having faith in him is the foremost step towards success.
We will achieve everything we want only if we will be truly blessed and away from stress.

Happiness will be in our way.
Miracles are just a prayer away.
In this world where people are now so fraud,
It's better for us to get close to God.

We have lost so much in this world, not realizing it will end one day
And we will left with nothing except our good deeds, so you need to just pray.

Pray with a clean soul, pure body and with a kind heart
Because praying is the most beautiful nature's art.

41

A WHISPER FROM WITHIN

Dr. Apteena Johnson Kakkadu

Take me with you, my Lord.
I found the prettiest vows
at my hardest times,
and yes,
I found God,

I've never seen him,
but I've felt him,
through faces,
through voices,
and through love.

He was never far,
but was supreme for everything beneath the earth.

Why did you die for me,
for this wicked, wretched, and dreadful soul,
my Lord...

Cause I am nothing, but a pinch
of misery and pain.
I could see darkness,
right within me.

But still, you delivered
 a ray of light in me,
How could you even forgive me lord,
I've brought disgrace to your name and glory.

Bring me back to you, my Lord.
Cause I am far away,
a place without a name,
but utter murk and evil shadows.

I couldn't even breathe,
Cause I'm strangled by
my sinful thoughts and doings.

Deliver me a ray of hope, my lord.
Cause I'm not worthy of any of it.
Come back to me lord,
embrace me with your love and care,

I'm here,
shattered and frazzled,
searching for your presence.

Take me back my lord,
take my soul,
to rest with you...

42

THROUGH A LITTLE GIRL'S EYES

Rebecca Nelson

I'm staring out of the window in front of the kitchen sink.

As I'm standing there, sobbing, I begin to rethink
Through a pair of little girl's eyes, so scared and alone.

Thinking nobody would ever really know
How hurting it is for her, how it felt to live with a lie.

It led her to wonder, is there really a Savior by my side?

If so, why are these things still happening, she would pray:
"Please, can you make the pain go away?"

She cries herself into a daze, only to be led into a nightmarish sleep.

And shudders as she remembers the anguish seemingly forever on
repeat:
"Hey Jesus, you're listening...right?
How long, do you think, until I'll finally be alright?"

43

YOUR PALE LEMON- YELLOW EYES

Sulagna Samanta

I have been walking through the lines,
Guarded by the old dusty pine.
In the middle of the night,
In search for your pale lemon-yellow eyes.

Had I not lost you in the maze
On that stormy day,
We could have measured many paths
Through the woods to the bay.

They call me with names like - mad, psycho and insane.
For they think I hallucinate you even in the darkest lane.
They sympathize but can't empathize with me,
Because you are just a four-pawed creature to them.
I pity them to not have a heart
To feel the love we share;
After all only I can feel your gaze,
Hear you 'm-e-o-w'
In a poised voice, there.

Oh, Simon! No longer play the hide and seek game with me,
No longer punish me for the mistake I've done.
For I know you are still alive,
Hiding from me and winning
Because you wear that black fur with pride.

Ah! There you are my love,
I knew you won't stay afar from me.
I had faith in how our hearts are aligned.
I knew you will forgive me,
I knew you will make a visit
From the blind spot that lies far there.

44

LIFE- A PUZZLE

Sistla Shravya

Life, what a beautiful puzzle, wanting you to be in a hustle .
Every piece lacking it's onism, still has its own selcouth.
What an aesthete He is, framing a perfect frame.
We got to know Him, still remains an orphic.
 Trying every single second making us realize to find not to fit.
Not to fit in others lacuna, instead find our own vie.
To find your paix, stop achieving their voeux.
A marahuyo will find his guapa.

45

HOW GREAT

Jagruthi Kommuri

How great is the creation,
That it reminds us the supremacy of the Creator;
How blessed are humans to feel something and be able to explain the
emotion,
That it helps us realize we are nothing but a handy work of the
Creator;
How the world works, this does not end in an explanation,
But it surely makes us discern the presence of the Creator;
Who are we to feel significant and live this generation,
Nothing but to praise how magnificent is the glory of the Creator.

46

THE FICTITIOUS FAITH

Shivani Sharma

The Day is climbing, I'm thinking.
River of believe is falling down,
From mountains over the lands.
Our ocean denies to get,
And that heaves.
Breathing morn of its greatest.
Supports beneath of me.
Or homely annals joys.
It's all about faith.
Daily overcoming with inevitable hour.
Has faith lost somewhere?
Why these hands are trembling for doing something for others?
Because evil minded don't take,
And others continue.
Has my soul stopped believing in faith?
No, I'm not someone who regrets.
But I believe on those who did for me.
People make sweet morn; some don't
Faith is constant, is it?

It is not manna dew, always.
Sometimes it is waste away.
Beware, take gentle thoughts.
Where it is not world despise.
Glorify, if globe trusts you.
And that circle of constant faith, glitters.
So why are you not thinking to do?
Make this blaze of light ever new.
Faith will never come to devil.
Hope, river of believe is not falling down
From mountains over the lands.
From crown to heels.

STORIES

1

JASMINE

Isidora Radovanac

At a time when the flourishing of culture, religion and customs was spreading throughout her humble, earthly life, marking the end of the 19th century and as the last rays of the sun were giving their bliss to the wooden roofs of Balkan villages, her curled figure, wrapped in dark, dusty cotton, was placed on a stump in front of the hut, trembling slightly. The cold of the coming winter showed no pity. The first snowflakes were expected at any moment. She persevered in the icy heat, which crept under her layers of cheap cloth. However, it has been a long time since she was lonely and thoughtful before one winter sunset. Behind the hut, the sky burned in a bright orange hue, interwoven with yellow beams of sunlight, which went to rest. Her white, frozen hands were busy weaving another pair of woolen gloves. This time, she tried to make them be in the full shape of the hand, carefully weaving the place where each finger will fit. She was finishing the palm of the left glove when she heard the carts approaching. She didn't have to look up from the handicraft to know whose they were. The familiar sound of rattling, creaking and sluggish hooves of two old mares briefly ripped her ears. Placing the mares in the barn, he called her by name to enter the hut. At that moment, she jerked out of the shallow half-sleep. She began to collect the remnants of red wool and weaving material, clutching it in her arms, and then, with a tormented walk, walked to the door. Only when she settled into a wooden chair by the stove and when she smelled the intoxicating scent of soup, which filled her nostrils with pleasure, she realized that she had spent the whole four hours weaving in front of the house. It was strange to her that she did not feel the slightest pain in her back, nor any sign of the passing of time, except for the fiery sunset, which she remembered. Swimming with memories from her youth, she watched indifferently her husband, who recounted his usual working day in the field, describing their beauty before sunset, which he listened to from the stories of others and which he could never see. He looked unsatisfactorily at the metal plate of soup in front of him, turning the spoon in his hand.

"It's not salty enough," he murmured, "your mother didn't teach you anything?

I'll have dinner in the field tomorrow. Everything is better than this pickled soup."

"Very well. Eating dinner, you will enjoy the sunset behind the miles of wheat, which you are so eagerly waiting to see", she answered coldly, without taking her eyes off her plate.

"You know, I shall," he replied.

Of course, he ate everything from the plate. A busy day has done its thing, it seems. As usual, he asked her about the work she was supposed to do and which she did in the morning, in order to dedicate the rest of the day to weaving, by habit.

"I managed to finish a pair of gloves for this winter today. I know you complained about the past ones, so I tried to make these thicker. Look", she said, pointing to him, "they also have room for each finger. I think it will suit you."

"Oh, wonderful. I have never seen anything more beautiful in my life", he said sarcastically, "I had the opportunity to meet ten-year-old girls with more skillful fingers. Look at these ornaments ... Completely irregular and impersonal."

She stood remorsefully by the bowl of warm water, scrubbing the plates, listening to the harsh words from his mouth. Rising from his chair, he passed her sullenly, deliberately pushing her on while walking. She continued to stare at the wounds on her hands, dipped in warm water with dirty plates. She still felt the pain of being hit with a belt, which was a punishment for an insufficiently clean work suit and a terribly bitter vegetable salad. Her moans that night played in the walls of the neighborhood's homes, which pitied her at every turn, cutting her husband's gaze. Height, size, and cruelty served him as an invisible weapon.

"What kind of woman are you?!", he shouted after the beatings,

"you are incapable of life! You don't know how to cook, you can't have children, the house has never been dirtier!

"But I cleaned today, I did everything", she said through tears.

"Is this a clean house for you?!" he shouted. He ran his fingers over the surface of the dresser. A thin layer of dust remained on his skin. He slapped her.

She remembered staying in the fetal position until morning, grunting and praying that God would take her. And now, she lays down in bed, next to the same man, watching with disgust his ugly, wide and sweaty face, the surface of which was hidden by a half-gray mustache. His nature had changed like his appearance, she thought. Thirty-three years ago, that face was much narrower and smoother, seductively pale. A neat, black mustache protected the softest lips, she remembered, and his black eyes floated through her body that night, the most beautiful night of her life. Then she thought she was glad they had forced her into marriage. At the age of fifty-one, she was a beautiful old woman, but she could not compare herself to an eighteen-year-old in white silk with flowing light brown hair, adorned with pearls and gold, hazel eyes, and smooth, fair skin as she stood before him ready for a wedding kiss. Is that the same man, she thought. Extinguishing the candle on the bedside table, she sank into sleep.

"Jasmine! Jasmine!", she heard an echo of her name.

She opened her eyes, but the voice disappeared. "Jasmine", the same voice whispered. She looked to her right and saw a beautiful, youthful woman with milky white skin, dark well-groomed hair, and blue eyes, clad in a velvet cloth. Her face radiated a faint light, which cleared the complete eclipse of the bedroom. The woman sat on the edge of the bed, leaning over, so that now the light of her face fell on Jasmine's, dancing in her hazel eyes like the flame of a candle.

"Who are you? What do you want?", Jasmine asked timidly.

"Do not be scared. The last thing I intend to do is hurting you."

"Who are you?"

"I thought you might want to talk to me. You see, your friends, family, and the man you gave your love to, for whom you sacrificed your precious virginity. They don't know about your pain. But Heaven knows, be assured. Every bit of suffering, every rush of hopelessness and hurt you felt, went through our heart."

"Ours? You are ... You are ...?"

"Yes, my dear. I am the one to whom so many prayers have been addressed over the centuries and through whose womb the most lovely, most sublime life came into the world as a gift of the Lord himself," she said in a gentle, soothing tone, "but right now that's none of importance. Listen to me, Jasmine. You must know that your suffering, like the suffering of any human being in this world, has its place in the scheme of things within God's plan. The Heaven has not turned its back on you, it sees and feels your pain. You have never been, nor will you ever be, unnoticed in the eyes of souls, saints, angels, my eyes, and the eyes of the Holy Trinity. Never.

Know that everyone will be responsible for their actions, if not on Earth, then before its Creator."

"Most Holy Mother of God, does that mean that I should obey his behavior? Do I have to suffer the blows with a belt and a whip for another twenty years, which is amount of time that's left to me for living on Earth, in order to be rewarded for my obedience with God's hand? How could someone who's religious be so cruel and insensitive to his wife and the environment?

He... He never helped any of his friends, even though they did help him. He has been abusing me for more than two decades. After our wedding, he became a different man. I can't recognize my husband, whom I have lived for thirty-three years with! And again, he regularly goes to the Sunday liturgy, takes communion, accepts the blood of Christ in his body and says "Our Father" three times a day, before each meal as a sign of gratitude. Whenever I want to defend myself against the accusations, he makes against me, he starts quoting the verses of the Holy Scriptures. 'It is better to live in a corner of the housetop than in a house shared with a quarrelsome wife' Or 'But I want you to understand that the head of every man is Christ, the head of a wife is her husband, and the head of Christ is God.' He beats me until I repeated that thought.

Ah, there's that verse: 'Let a woman learn quietly with all submissiveness. I do not permit a woman to teach or to exercise authority over a man; rather, she is to remain quiet. For Adam was formed first, then Eve; and Adam was not deceived, but the woman was deceived and became a transgressor. Yet she will be saved through childbearing — if they continue in faith and love and holiness, with self-control. 'Holy Mother, I'm begging you, tell me, is it really the Christian duty of a woman to be oppressed and devoted to her husband, is he really the master of her body?"

The Mother of God sighed slightly, continuing: "The world was emerging gradually. The Revelations of evolution lasted for millions of years, while the angels watched them with enthusiasm, sending melodies of praise and exaltation to the Lord. The Heavens roared from the divine, pure sopranos, who came from the throats of God's angels themselves, his closest spiritual beings. Together they observed the Earth, its development, the development of the world and, finally, the human race. First, the tiniest bases of matter became organic, making up what English scientists called cells. Hereditary traits soon developed, fluids that accelerated and stimulated the process of progress, multicellular living organisms, greenery, and the first animals were created. Even when time led to the moment of observing death and decay, most angels knew that it was a part of nature, of God's hands, and that one must die for the life of another. The Lord asked only a small number of angels, who could not bear the sounds of suffering and the sight of the dying of living beings, to have confidence in Him, because He knew what He was doing. And He wants the same thing from people today; from people whose cries no one but Him hears. Find some place in your heart to forgive your Creator, Jasmine. You will be saved." "Yes," she said quietly, "I will, of course I will. People are the one who bring evil to this world after all. But I must ask you again, Most Holy Mother of God, what am I to do next during the remaining years of this life? Is it a sin to fight for yourself if you are a woman?"

"The world has been enriched by the development and arrival of new beings. Nature was adorned with the colors of flowers, while the leading role was played by the encephalization of living beings, the first skeletons and nervous systems appeared. Then came the recognition of the face by the image of God - two eyes, a nose, a mouth. Through the time of giant reptiles and the appearance of insects, warm-blooded birds, mammals, a modern man soon walked the Earth, apelike haired and stooped, with a face even more similar to God's. When female started to look more distinctly than male and when the evolution led to the appearance of different eye and hair color, the world started to resemble today's." "But your story is completely different from the creation of the world described in the Holy Bible," said Jasmine. "Yes. The Holy Scriptures were written by man's hand, his mind, understanding and perception of experience, that is the Epiphany. People who were chosen by the Lord to experience and see His vision developed their own theories over time and wrote them down. Those who experienced so-called supernatural experiences attributed them to the Lord. Then, people who suffered from various apparitions due to illness, the mentally ill... It was believed that such apparitions were true Epiphanies and that the Lord provided hints about Himself and Heaven through them, and a final record called the Bible was created. That is the reason why it explains many things that never happened, many incorrect conclusions and unrealistic theories, because of which many people will lose faith or have lost it. But you will not lose it, Jasmine, because now you know the truth ", she made a short pause, "He is not only in Heaven, on his Most Holy Throne. He is in front of your hut, in it, here in the room, next to you and me, with your neighbors, friends and enemies."

"I understand. He is everywhere, and it is the Holy Spirit who brings His energy to Earth." The Virgin nodded. "So, science and faith should go hand in hand? Because people are researching natural phenomena and turning them into science, while these phenomena are God's handiwork, aren't they?" "Exactly. I think you can now answer the question you asked me yourself."

"Yes, Most Holy Mother of God. Incorrect writings in the Bible, which resulted from insufficient knowledge and wrong beliefs of individuals, determined the position and role of women in society. Based on her ability to give birth, care for children and much greater empathy than a man, she is characterized as a weaker, lower being, whose destiny is to be under the rule of her stronger half. That's why all women are in lower positions, isn't it? And such a system was created by humanity in the belief that it is God's will.

A smile now shone on the Virgin's face. Her face radiated warmth. "No, it is not wrong for a woman to work in the field, drink a well-deserved jug of cold beer, or have a greater desire to contribute to the world than to run a household. In ancient times, when the world was just evolving, men hunted and fought for the survival of the family because God made them physically stronger. In today's times, especially in the future, human life will be much more valued, and luxury will belong to everyone. The development of the society will progress even more, as will the industry. Men and women have long since made enough progress to declare equality."

"Then why have they not?" "Habits, customs and lifestyles cannot be changed easily and quickly. Unfortunately, the rest of your life will not change in that point, however, the lives of future women shall. They will gather the courage to seek justice", said the Mother of God with a warm smile, which still did not leave her face. She put her palm on Jasmin's cheek, continuing: "Please, do not rebel against a bitter life of yours. You will spend a few more years within your miserable, torturous life, and then, if the lovely Lord, our Creator and Almighty decides so, your soul will belong to the peace and abundance of the Kingdom of Heaven, the glorious empire of God. Be patient, persevere.

Leave the fight to future generations."

"How many people were honored to be in your presence?", Jasmine asked.

"Not much," she replied, smiling, "one of those of purer hearts and special thoughts."

"Please don't leave me," Jasmine whispered.

"As for your husband, I would say the Lord does not hear his prayers, in the true sense of the word."

"How so?"

"They're empty. Wordless." The Virgin's hand slowly moved from Jasmine's face. "I have to go now. I hope you will take my advice. Whatever you do, don't lose your faith. He is near you, next to you and He wants you to try to feel His presence, so remember that you are never truly alone. Never. And don't forget that we know about your pain, believe me, we feel it with the same strength. I love you, Jasmine."

The beautiful figure of the Blessed Virgin has faded.

The bedroom was lost in the darkness again. Jasmine sat up and rubbed her face lightly with her hands as if washing herself. Looking out the window, she saw rays of the rising sun, which paints the sky in incredible refracting shades of yellow, pink and dark blue until today, marking the visit of the Blessed Virgin Mary at the time of every beginning of the new winter in this humble village of Balkan.

2

THE ISRAELI SEIGE SCENE N°12: HIDING AT ZELDA'S PLACE

Sam Julio Fortes Neves

IDF Soldiers and captives can faintly be heard marching outside in a distance.

At a mid-tempo, but aggressive and authoritative pace, the IDF soldiers marched and could be heard synchronously with indiscriminate sounds of screams of dragged people and struggles. It does appear as if the sounds are closing in, as time swiftly progresses.

In a secret room behind the cabinet in Zelda's house Zahra, her son Ismail, her sister in law, Asiya and her baby daughter Layla, spent the night hiding. They attempted to make their escape at dawn. They were tormented by something that was a distant imaginative nightmare to some, but the reality they experienced. The anxious feelings made its way through their mental state. The despair and fear, seeped through their veins, it was carried by their nerves as they heavily perceived of what was occurring outside. They were well aware of the consequence of getting caught.

The sounds were heard by all who were present, raising the tension in the confined space. Except for Layla who was fast asleep for the time being. Zahra and Asiya, both understood that those were the sounds of patrolling IDF soldiers making their rounds. Zelda got up from her chair to close the curtains while she simultaneously turned on the volume of the television to camouflage any potential sound. The Israelian news could be heard from the living room.

Then she walked over to the cabinet and gently knocked thrice on an antique teacup, and corresponding spoon, with a recognizable tone and cadence she said: "Zahra, do not worry yourself, I can hear them in a distance, remain as calm as possible, we'll be fine if they do not hear us. We are in this together, okay?"

"Shoukran! Zelda, I do not know, how I ever could repay you, Zahra whispered grateful and anxious at the same time.

"Already paid in full, we are family, I hope with Elohim's will, we will be spared from this situation." Zelda whispered with a tone of comfort and good faith.

"Insha Allah", Zahra whispered, conformingly with a hopeful tone. "Just hope we will be spared from a fate a lot of our loved ones had to suffer". Zelda whispered with her hand pressed against the handle of the cabinet and ensured the lock was on and out of plain sight.

"Okay, I'll have to go back now, keep your tones down if you can." Zelda then walked over to the living room whilst closing off all the lights.

Zahra and Asiya replied, in a whispering matter: "Shoukran Zelda."

They are ethnically cleansing the area, as we speak , Zahra thought to herself. She saw that her child beared a scared expression on his face, she then comfortingly said: "Don't be scared my child, we'll be safe if they do not hear us." Whilst she tried to undertone her own fears.

"Where is Baba?" Ismaïl asked worrisome, as he pointed towards the door, which was barricaded by the cabinet. "Is Baba outside Mama?"

"Papa will be back soon, habibi, don't worry. Papa is out with uncle Zohair, to help uncle Seraphine with an errand. They will be back" she said with a sure tone.

Try to get some sleep we have to get up early in the morning, Insha Allah, Baba will be back tomorrow, okay?"

"Insha Allah!", Ismaïl said, as Zahra tucked him into bed. "Why are we hiding from soldiers mama, did we do something wrong?", Ismaïl asked.

"We opened our borders when they did not have a place to call home. Whilst we were willing to share, they want to claim it as their own." Zahra said as she looked around in the dark room, solemnly litten by a few candles.

"Not all Jews are bad people right mama?" Ismail asked semirhetorical, with an innocent smile.

Reassuring, Zahra said "Exactly habibi, there are Jewish people that fight for the same cause, like Aunt Zelda and uncle Seraphine. There are good and bad people everywhere." As she kissed Ismaïl on his forehead.

"There is a group of people... with evil intentions, but I will teach you all about it, when the time will come, Insha Allah. As of now, you are still too young to understand, you are a bright boy, but... The time will come, Insha Allah, that you will be able to comprehend." Asiya felt a sense of comfort as she saw the beautiful bond between Zahra and Ismaïl. She recognized that even in the most barren situations there still reside blessings from the Lord, for those who see at least.

"Okay?" Zahra asked ensuring. "Oke, mama." Ismaïl affirmed and turned over to his sleeping side.

"Good, well go to sleep habibi", Zahra said while she kissed Ismaïl on his forehead.

Zahra spent a few minutes listening to the dreadful news and simultaneously processed it in thought, whilst she wandered visually in the dark corner of the room. Meanwhile, Asiya was looking at Zahra and wondered what she was thinking about. She herself was concerned with what she heard on the news. After a while she looked at her baby with a bittersweet expression, as she had thoughts of concerns about the future predicament.

Then, Zahra shoved over to Asiya, who was still rocking and

looking at her baby. "We are hiding in our own country", Zahra whispered, "being hunted down and wiped from the world map, for no justifiable reason. Just for being us."

The stomping of combat boots passing around the corner could be heard and the screaming back and forth between the captives and the soldiers also became louder.

Asiya looked up facing Zahra.

Zahra then continued "It's a shame, we could peacefully coexist. We are innocent, I would never hurt a fly." Zahra whispered to Asiya. "All I ever wanted was, for my children to have a safe future." Asiya nods, expressing feelings of mutual understanding.

A strong contrast is painted in the atmosphere as their emotions that consisted of intrinsic purity are in constant flux with the invading extrinsic reality.

On the other side of the wall the reverberation of sounds from across the street could be heard. The sounds of the IDF soldiers and the captives became a lot clearer as they passed by the latitude of the secret room. Trying to ignore the happening phenomena outside, Zahra then again, for a brief moment, focused on the spot, not struck by light, in the corner of the ceiling which was dark and boundless due to the darkness. Amidst the moment while she gazed into the darkness, she said "to feel welcomed on this planet, like they should be", Zahra whispered, expressing a feeling of incomprehension, as she kept staring.

"Be patient, Zahra, for Allah does not sleep, is just, and is a witness over all things." Asiya said with an ascertaining tone. "I will never forget that you taught me this and I will carry this unto my grave. I will always be grateful for what you taught and..."

Zahra turned her head and whispered: "I know, Asiya, I am just concerned. I don't know if we will make it alive?" Zahra expressed in a state of anxiety. "Something just doesn't feel right."

"Do not lose faith in Allah, let us pray for our salvation, and make extra dua. Asiya said with a comforting smile, whilst firmly holding Zahra's hand.

Zahra got up to get their prayer mats and Asiya got up to put Layla in the cradle. Zahra tried to hand over Asiya's prayer mat, while Asiya bended over to put Layla inside of it. The IDF soldiers and captives could be heard coming to a standstill. Zelda notices and walks over to the window and peeps through a small hole in the curtain. A loud smack to the face was heard as someone loudly hit the ground.

"Get up!" The Israelian soldier yelled at the fallen captive, "Or I will put you out of your misery, and it'll be my pleasure", he continued.

Both Zahra and Asiya where silenced by a terrorizing feeling of fear. They were looking at each other distraught and terrified. Whilst on her knees a wailing woman was heard outside: "Lā ilāha il- Allah, Lā ilāha il- Allah, Lā ilāha il- Allah". Zahra and Asiya both flinched, sweating with moist hands due to the nerves. Distraught with the situation, in a flight response, they slowly crept over to the crawl space. An IDF soldier cocked his gun. "Is that Fatima?" Asiya alarmed as she pressed Layla against herself.

"Lā ilāha Il-Allah..."

A trigger was pulled, two shots could be heard, the latter being a kill confirmation. In between shots, Zelda looked away in state of trauma, but yet concerned looked at the cabinet. She silently walked over to the chair in front of the television. Ismaīl was startled awake by the sound, in a state of confusion. In an automatic response Zahra and Asiya covered their own and their children's mouth, to make sure they were kept unheard.

Outside, the IDF Soldiers could be heard giving radio relay. "Alpha... this is Bravo I think the perimeter is clear, suggesting meeting at checkpoint Charlie...."

Asiya's baby starts crying.

3

IN GOD'S IMAGE

Manoj Vaz

Unnikrishnan Nair waited restlessly as the Customs Officer accosted him on the way out of the green channel at the international airport in Mumbai and directed him to a corner where he and a fellow officer started rummaging through his small suitcase.

"Idiots..." Unni murmured, "let them make a fool of themselves!"

Unni realized that the fact that he had only a small suitcase with him on a New York-Mumbai flight must have raised their hackles. He was unperturbed, there were only some used clothes in the suitcase and the only things of value, his personal MacBook, and the bottle of Macallan Single Malt he had purchased at the JFK duty free shop were in his hand baggage. But then, he had declared both in the declaration form and he was not liable to pay customs duty for either.

Unni was coming to India after 8 years. He didn't have any relatives in India to get any gifts for. His mother had died when he was in his teens and his dad a few years later when he was in his final year of mechanical engineering at the Regional Engineering College in Calicut.

While most of his colleagues attempted GRE in a bid to do Master's in Engineering with full scholarship in the US, Unni had concentrated on GMAT. He understood he would not get a scholarship from the Ivy League institutes but he had a plan.

Unni's genius was never in doubt. He had scored 169 in the IQ test conducted in his engineering college and was an active member of the international high IQ society MENSA.

"Use your intelligence well", his quantum physics teacher had advised him, "Einstein only had IQ of 160."

After topping GMAT, he had applied to only two colleges, Harvard, and Stanford. Stanford rejected him and Harvard accepted him, without scholarship.

As planned, he quickly sold off the 20 acres of prime land that was passed on to him from his father and secured admission.

"Who wants to live in this God forsaken country?!" He had sworn then.

And here he was 8 years later, smiling magnanimously at the disappointed Customs Officer as handed him his suitcase and apologized for the inconvenience caused.

In the five years he spent in Lindt, Morgan & Anderson, considered by most advertising pundits as the bête noire of Madison Avenue, he had strategized umpteen marketing successes. Now he was ready for the ultimate test of his genius.

He was all set to create God.

He had been planning it for the last two years and had all ends sewn up in his mind. He had also saved up 2,50,000 USD to invest in the project.

Before coming down to India, he had contacted a real estate agent and taken a furnished bungalow in suburban Mumbai on Leave & License for 11 months. The agent had been informed of his arrival and was told to open the bungalow and wait for him so that he could take the prepaid cab from the airport straight to his new abode.

Once he signed the deed and paid off the beaming agent, he opened the bottle of Macallan and made himself a drink and settled down. The bungalow was too big for him, but he saw it bristling with people in his mind; it was exactly what he required.

The next day he cabbed it to Colaba in downtown Mumbai. He had a meeting set up with another 'agent' at Leopold Bar and Restaurant. His brief to the agent was simple; he needed a six to eight foreigners, women more than men, who would be in Mumbai for six months at least. Addiction to mild drugs like Marijuana, Hashish was okay but not chemical drugs.

The agent had carried a pocket album and showed him photos of a couple of dozen 'eligible' foreigners with their brief CVs. Unni shortlisted about 15 of them and asked for a personal interview with each.

"How much will you pay them per month?" Asked the agent.

"Rs. 25,000 per month plus stay and food." Replied Unni.

"And me?" The agent smiled displaying his crooked teeth.

"10% of the total monthly payroll and if you join us as coordinator, the pay will continue for 6 months…" Unni continued, "I will be away for the weekend, make sure the personal meetings start on Monday!"

The same evening, he boarded a train for Ratnagiri, a coastal district of Maharashtra. His best friend's father was a senior bureaucrat in the district, he had been assured of all the help he needs.

The train was too dirty for his liking, the artificial woolen blankets were itchy, and the jet lag kept him awake, but Unni was a man on a mission. These were nothing but minor distractions in a higher cause.

He reached the palatial bungalow of the Deshmukhs just in time for breakfast. Deshmukh senior welcomed him and put his nephew Jayesh at his service.

"Jayesh knows the area well, he will drive you around; you can take the SUV and don't worry, anything you want can be arranged. I am the king of this jungle!" The old man laughed.

Straightaway after breakfast, Unni proceeded with Jayesh to meet the schoolteachers in the district. Being a Saturday, most of them were at home.

The conversations were almost repetitive. After introducing himself and exchanging pleasantries, Unni would enquire if the teacher had come across any specific children who looked normal but had learning difficulties?

Unni struck gold with the third teacher they met.

Sixteen-year-old Kamli was a dyslexic girl who quit school in the fourth grade. Medium height, fair complexioned, plump and moon faced, Kamli was exactly what Unni had in his mind.

Her parents were poor laborers who thought maybe she could earn a living as a domestic help. But Kamli refused. All day she would sit on the riverbank and play with kids half her age. So, when Unni offered them Rs. 50,000 to take Kamli away and help her earn a respectable living, they happily relented. Their only concern was her safety, which Unni allayed by agreeing to take her older brother Raju along with her.

The next day, Unni took the train back to Mumbai along with Kamli and Raju. Along the way he explained to both what their roles would be. Once back in Mumbai, he quickly selected eight foreigners, six among them women, to be part of his coterie.

Next, he contacted a leading Public Relations firm and after getting them to sign a confidentiality agreement, briefed them of his requirement.

"This girl, Kamli, is a Goddess incarnate" he explained, "She will be henceforth known as Mata Sarvahiteshwari. I want you to spin out articles about her mysterious background and her spiritual powers of healing and cleansing souls. I want every newspaper and every news channel to cover her emergence."

While the PR agency got into the act, Unni's rented bungalow became a beehive of activity. The eight foreigners, Kamli and Raju were given a month-long crash course in religious discourses, Sanskrit shlokas along with yoga and meditation. All of them were given made to order traditional saffron robes, only Kamli was given a white cotton saree to make her stand apart. The men were also encouraged to refrain from shaving so that they looked their part. All the foreigners and Raju were given Sanskrit names befitting sadhus and sadhvis.

By then articles started appearing in mainline newspapers about the young God incarnate called Mata Sarvahiteshwari by her loving devotees. Stories about her extraordinary healing powers with a simple touch started making rounds.

Unni rented a minibus and started taking the coterie to the homes of rich and influential people. Pamphlets were distributed publicizing the visit and people began to visit her. Donations were solicited for Mata Sarvahiteshwari's dream of building an ashram and school for children.

Unni had already registered the Mata Sarvahiteshwari Trust in Ratnagiri with the help of Mr. Deshmukh there. Since he was an American citizen, he made Kamli Rane aka Mata Sarvahiteshwari, the chairman of the trust with a year-long Power of Attorney, empowering Unni to manage the funds and sign on all documents including cheques.

"But I don't have any powers..." Kamli complained, "Shouldn't I, at least, learn a few magic tricks like some of the other God men?"

"You don't need to." replied Unni, "Just hug your devotees and say whatever they want will be done. People try every possible means to get work done, but if it gets done, the credit always goes to God!" and steadily, Mata Sarvahiteshwari's followers grew.

She was constantly in the news and TV channels followed her. Top politicians and film stars sought her blessings. The coffers of Mata Sarvahiteshwari Trust started swelling. In less than a year, the corpus had touched 75 crore rupees.

Unni and his team, zeroed in a fifty-acre seaside plot in Sindhudurg District near Ratnagiri to build their ashram and school. It was a mega project that would cost over 60 crore rupees to complete. A token amount was paid to the landowner to confirm the deal and building plans and elevations were drawn up.

Only problem was that Unni had other plans in mind. He had succeeded in creating God and now was getting bored and claustrophobic in the saffron robe and beard.

A day before his power of attorney expired, he planned to transfer the funds to his bank in the Cayman Islands and scoot from the country. He had it planned to perfection. Tickets were booked, visa and all arrangements done. Moreover, his contract with the trust had been worded in a way that he could not be touched without implicating the whole team.

Two days before the Power of Attorney expired, Unni strode into the bank and filled out and signed the documents for the transfer of funds. The pretty young assistant manager then went inside to get the required approvals from the General Manager.

A little later, Unni was called into the General Manager's cabin.

"Mr. Nair," the old man said in a somber voice, "I am afraid I cannot comply with your request."

"Why so?" Demanded Unni indignantly.

"Because your power of attorney has been revoked by Ms. Kamli Rane, just yesterday. You are no longer the authorized signatory of the Mata Sarvahiteshwari Trust."

The General Manager showed Unni the document that bore Kamli's thumb print, which clearly stated that Raju Rane would be the authorized signatory of the trust henceforth.

Furious, Unni stormed out of the bank to confront Kamli. When he reached the gate, he realized that the security had been replaced. And the new guards had been instructed not to let him in.

Unni was smart enough to realize that he was beaten.

And there he was on the Mumbai - New York flight, his dream realized yet shattered. All the while trying to figure out how a genius like him could be outsmarted by an illiterate young village belle?

The timing of her counter action was too perfect to be true. Did she read the treachery in his mind?

Had he, succeeded in creating... God?

4

A DREAM CALLED FAITH

Kaitlyn Leiva

I dreamed I was trapped in a world full of sadness. Everyone was broken and sad, waiting to truly smile. They had hollow faces and looked like skulls. I witnessed fake smiles and forced laughs. Everyone tried to look like the sad woman or man on the cover of the magazines. I saw war and destruction everywhere on the news.

"Breaking News from Yemen, the country the world failed," the monotone voice boomed.

"Breaking News: another innocent, unarmed man killed today by police during a peaceful protest."

Conflict and death were the norm. The people lived in fear of their impending doom. They lived believing there was no hope for them. This was not about living anymore, it was about surviving.

I dreamed I was a sinful soldier, with no hope of the afterlife. I would blindly go, murder, return to the safety of my home. I felt that humanity was hopeless, and I was unsalvable. I was another piece in this giant chess game called life. At the end of the day, my family and I were getting paid and would go another month without being homeless.

In this dream, I found myself in battle on the losing team. The ruins of a country long forgotten around me. With every step, I found myself haunted by the fallen around me. The constant berating sound of gunfire surrounded me. The bullets whizzed by me. They were too close for comfort, but what is comfortable about a war? About killing people fighting for their country?

It was a lost cause. There was no winning in this battle. There was no happy ending. It was do or die.

I found myself dropping my weapon and sinking to my knees. I did something humankind had long forgotten to do. I prayed. I prayed for peace. I prayed for love. I prayed for humanity. I prayed for redemption and forgiveness. I prayed with everything I was, tears flowing in streams down my cheeks. I cried out in misery the prayers of my heart.

I dreamed of a miracle. Every soldier, one by one, dropped their weapon. They turned their faces to the bleak sky and prayed, tears flowing down their faces. Prayers in every language circled around me. I dreamed that my tears of fear and grief became those of elation. I dreamed our tears touched the sand, and the sand became grass. The people hiding in collapsed buildings came out of their house to see why the gunfire had come to a sudden cessation. They sobbed and sunk to their knees as well.

I dreamed that thousands of miles away in the city I had called home, my mother was watching the news with my children as their father endured another day at the jobs, he had to put his mind at ease. She had the same empty expression as she sat aimlessly in front of the television.

"Breaking news: soldiers overseas drop their weapons for a moment of prayer and peace for the world."

My mother became animated and called anyone she knew. She told them to turn on the news. She dropped to her knees and she prayed as well. She was grateful and she was crying tears of joy.

Soon the whole battlefield was made of grass. The buildings were rebuilt. Families were reunited. Mothers and fathers were crying seeing their sons and daughters returning to them, wives and husbands wept as their partners ran to them and held them close, and children looked to their parents with tears in their eyes and pride in their hearts. They cried but they were not sad. They were not heartbroken. They were relieved and hopeful.

I found my husband, my mother, and my children awaiting me with smiles on their faces. They stood before me, older than I last saw them, and realized how long I had been missing from their lives. I was not sad. I sent a prayer to the Lord expressing my gratitude.

Every soldier there then shook the hands of their enemies who became their brethren. We had all forgiven and began to love one another rather than holding onto hate.

I stood in awe of the beauty of peace, and the feeling of hope. I was overwhelmed with emotions, and I knew I had been saved. I dropped to my knees and prayed, but this time it was a prayer of gratitude and praise.

In this dream, I shivered due to the sheer power of God. He had heard our calls for help and need for change. Our prayers were so loud and so pure in intent. I was rendered unafraid. I was not depressed. My body and soul was full. The world had finally been fed what it needed all along: faith.

5

LIFE, STRUGGLES AND FAITH

Divyansh Dwivedi

Spiritualism, faith and devotion were the things Rakesh never used to believe in. Ramnagar village was treating him well, a dairy shop with a good earning, a beautiful wife, and a generous son.

One day, when he was getting ready to follow his daily routine of going to his shop, he indulged into a fight with his wife. His violent acts on his wife lead to a pathetic communication gap between them which became the reason for their separation.

Life for Rakesh became miserable. Loneliness was eating him from inside. Alcohol and suicidal thoughts were now a part of his daily life. His wife and son were no longer with him. He only had himself. He was now a soul that was broken and shattered. He was incapable to negotiate between needing to be connected and needing tension to be a distinct individual.

When he didn't find any answer to his problems, he chose the path of faith. Willing to embrace the healing of a broken heart and making an incomplete life complete he made faith his accomplice. Faith made him believe that how our souls are connected to our hearts and how the need of them to be interconnected is crucial. Once a non-believer of faith was now turning into a believer of faith. He started believing in God, spiritualism and faith was something he counted on. His struggles to find faith made him realize how blessed he was when his wife and son were with him and now nothing feels same, but faith has magic, a magic that can heal a broken soul.

Rakesh's beliefs in faith made him realize how his actions had an impact on others' lives. His life was slowly coming back on track. He used to go to his shop, his earning was increased. He was filled with positive thoughts. There were times when he used to think about his wife and son who once were a part of his happy life. With tears rolling down and heart skipping a beat he used to relive those moments, his sons voice calling him babuji, his wife's cherubic smile.

With each passing day, his thoughts made him think about how life can be unpredictable at the most unpredictable times. How struggles and faith in fighting with those hardships helps you to grow. Purity has a habit of coming back and when it joins faith, the person becomes the best version of himself.

Rakesh's struggles and mistakes tried to tear him apart. His faith in god, his faith in himself was what kept him going and fighting with every battle. Despite the doubts, faith in god, spiritualism is something to rely on. Rakesh made this line as his mantra to live his life to the fullest.

He was happy, enlightened, and thankful to the faith he adapted, he was living a life that only included love, positivity, and happiness.

He was happy, maybe more than he has ever been.

6

A CRACK IN THE SICILIAN REFLECTION N°8: UNPLEASANT REMEMBERANCE

Sam Julio Fortes Neves

As the Capo di Capi Franklin and his loyal right hands, Johnny and Victor sit by themselves in his near empty loft, they had a confidential conversation, in a confidential location. Discussing events that happened in the past. Victor and Johnny are helping Franklin to remember events, which Franklin seemed to have forgotten due to his dementia. The full moon shined bright through the big windows of the loft. As the light of one lamp swayed across the room it automatically created a grim setting. As the conversation started lightly, the tensions soon started to rise.

"I took a detour", Franklin pronounced after exhaling. Victor smiled with a nod:

"So, that's what took you so long, boss?"

Franklin said grinningly: "Ahha, Johnny! I was looking for this special type of restaurant, downtown." Whilst pressing the bud in the ashtray. "Couldn't find it anywhere", Franklin proclaimed smiling.

"All these new joints...Little Italy isn't, what it was aye, you know that Johnny?"

As Franklin stared into the evaporating smoke he said: "It's just... these fumes always remind me of this place where they served this special cannoli." Franklin laughed on a nostalgic pretense.

Franklin grabbed a new Mayan Cigar out of the box and put the cigar between his lips.

"Back when smoking was legal in public spaces, those were the good old days, huh, Johnny?" he said with a crooked smile and lighted the cigar. Franklin coughed heavily, whilst exhaling.

"You should consider quitting with the smoking, boss. They are bad for your health anyway and Little Italy, better yet New York, still needs you!"

"Aahhhh!" Franklin grunts with an innocent smirk, as the light sways like a pendulum over the Capo di Capi's semi-enlightened silhouette.

"These lungs aren't as vital as they were a long time ago Johnny, my day might come anytime soon."

As Franklin tried to get up from the chair, he said: "But help me remind me, aye Vic, my memory is failing me."

Victor lending an arm for support, whilst having a bittersweet expression.

Johnny said ascertained: "I think you mean La Bella Ferrara on 195 Grand street, boss?"

"Yes! Aahhh, La Bella Ferrara, opened since 1892, if I remember correctly, I will never forget Antonnio's Cannoli haha!" Franklin exclaimed in a state of rejoice as he started to remember. "Yes, you never fail me Johnny, never have!"

"Just like your father, he was the best friend a man could wish for himself, honestly." Franklin said as he walked over to the desk and picked up the frame. He pointed at the picture, with on it, a photo of Johnny's late father.

"I swear that on the Virgin Mary", he said. "Gone too soon but he died for the family, a real man I always say. You don't find them like that no more...."

Franklin looked at Vic and pointed at the picture, "don't you agree, Vic?"

Franklin mumbled something incomprehensible, with the Mayan Cigar still in between his lips.

"Such good memories are hard to forget, anyway", Franklin then said while he bluntly stared in front of him, with a glaze in his eyes.

Victor tried to remind Franklin as he said: "Did Vito and his goonies not ransacked that place, padrone, a long while ago? 'That filthy illegal peasant, contandino, did what?!'"

Franklin then started to curse instinctively in Sicilian. His dialect then became so strong it could be pin pointed, precisely to which neighbourhood he originated from.

"What happened to the owners, Johnny?" Franklin asked with an astonished expression.

Victor interjected quickly, looking respectfully to the ground. "they fatally got shot with a 12-gauge, boss...".

As the Capo di Capi looked astonished towards Johnny for confirmation. Johnny confirmed with a gloomy expression, which was intensified by the contrast in shadow of the swaying light in the room.

"...Ribcage blown out to the waist down, it is sad to say but sometimes I think it's better not to remember, capo", Victor said, while he tried to calm the nerve-struck Frank down.

Whilst still under the influence of the nerves Franklin asked in a semi-screamed volume: "How long have you known about this Vic?"

"Well sir Capo, it has been a while now." Vic said while he tried to undertone his traumatic experience. And took on his poker face as the right hand of Capo di Capi ought to do.

Franklin smashed madly on the table, "If I get my hands on that filthy dog, before God takes me from this earth, by another, I..."

Johnny listened, whilst having an expression of concern on his face.

But then Franklin turned around, "Hmmm, Cane...", Franklin walked slowly towards the window with one hand on his walking cane and one hand behind his back, he said: "I mean, Johnny, come on aye?"

He looked out of the window, with a sense of pride in his voice, only a real Sicilian patriot could have had and said: "What Italian? Even a Napolitano for Christ's sake, with a little bit of self-respect, murders an innocent and earnest man and his family for mere jest, this dastard bastard has no backbone, no morals!"

Franklin turned his face exposing his cheeks semi-lightened, the contrast showed his signs of aging very well, and said fervently: "Let alone honor, values or dignity! 'He looked down and said: "It used to be all about respect!", while yet again he lighted the cigar.

As Franklin coughed and breathed heavily, "You okay boss?" John asked perturbed.

"Yes, call me Franky will ya?" Franklin said with a comforting tone and smile, like a suffering but seasoned elderly capo often did. "I'm okay Johnny."

"Where is the buffoon hiding?" Franklin said while he brought his index finger to his lip. Franklin struggled to remember Vito's last known location, to his knowledge.

"He is already whacked", John said which brought Franklin to a short flinch, followed by "boss, by..."

Franklin then excited, by intrigue, interceded: "What goes around comes around, aye Johnny! 'Was it one of our boys Vic? Who sacked the porco, aye?" He said with a smirk on his face, which gave away that he could easily fill a hundred pages or more on diverse ending scenarios related to the probable cause of Vito's death.

Franklin said, whilst licking his lips: "Well spit it out aye!" Curious and excited at the same time. "Who sacked the maiale, spill the beans Johnny, come on?" He said whilst turning around and rubbing his hands.

"You did, boss?" Victor said concerned.

Franklin turned silent, obviously he was in a state of shock as he vaguely remembered a short vision of the cold-blooded murder. The anxious feeling of relapsing emotions retrieved from lost memories flushed the Capo di Capi straight red.

John directly followed, "It was you boss, he had what was coming to him, he threatened the fam...!"

"What!" Franklin asked, confused.

Cigar drops.

7

MY FAITH IN GOD

Shomama Islam

I'm a girl who has a strong belief in God. I have kept all of my hope and faith in God. Though, I'm just 16 years old, I do not have much life experiences but today I'm going to share how God is the most important part of our lives.

My belief says that God is the one who created us and for him we shall live. From the very starting, or it would be not wrong if I would say from the day I was born, God has remained my everything. My hope, my power, my best friend, my faith, my guide, my happiness, my joy, my love, and my family. He gave me life, he gave me the opportunity to live a beautiful life crested by him.

God is the one, the Almighty, the creator of everything as well as the destroyer too.

I saw people talking that it is difficult for them to have believe in something which they cannot see, but they must not forget that God is the giver as well as the taker of our lives. He made us a human, with a heart pumping blood, a mind working all day, eyes to see, ears to hear and much more. We aren't created on our own, he is the one who created us and everything on this earth.

Because of him we breath, he gives us happiness and countless blessings. Though, he also gives us tears and sadness but also teaches us that "Rainbow is made after little Rain." He gives us tough situations to test us, to check whether we are getting closer to him or not as he is always waiting for us to ask, to ask whatever we want from and to pray. The God Says, "Call upon me, I'll surely respond you."

Today, we humans are lost so much in our own activities that we don't have time to worship God. I feel really sad when I see people don't have time for the one who created us. We are so busy in our lives, we have made our schedule so hectic and our routines too busy that our faith in God is slowly diminishing and that is the reason why today most of us are not familiar with inner peace because inner peace can only be found in God.

I see a lot of people are not praying, and those who are praying they are pretending more than praying. They don't pray with a pure heart. Their body may be physically present there but mentally they keep on thinking about something else. I also see few people being so selfish that they only remember God when they want something from him and when God accepts their prayers and gives them happily whatever they want, they don't even realize to thank him once. They forget to say thank you to the one who made it possible for them to let things happen.

It is also very easy to question him, to question about his existence, to question him if something goes wrong, to blame him, to question him when he is not listening to our prayers, but ever we had a question for ourselves?

Why my prayers are not being accepted? Have I made any mistake? Is God angry with me? Why is he delaying my prayers? Is he having better plans for me?

Ask one question to yourself before arising a question for God, the Almighty. The people who questioned him are the ones who don't appreciate the things they are blessed with.

Whatever God does, he does it for a reason, for our betterment and for our benefit.

God never denies any of our prayers, he answers to our prayers in three ways -

*He says, "Yes."

*He says, "Very soon, have patience."

*Or he says, "I have a better plan for you."

So, whatever decision he makes, He makes it for a reason. We should be patient, and should keep faith in him.

As a good human, we must show our humanity, our concern towards nature, towards people, and must be kind to each living soul on the earth. The world will end one day, and we'll be left with nothing, except our good deeds, kind nature and good behavior.

God never does anything wrong with us, and all we need to do is obey him, go on the right path, follow the instructions he gives, be a good human, be thankful to him, keep believing in him, have faith, patience, and hope. You will have a truly blessed life, on the earth and thereafter.

8

THE MIRACLE LOVE YOU NEED

Rosanna Purkiss

A relationship with God is many things. It's a kind of love you will never get from anyone. No one. Not even your mum, your dad, your partner, or your best friend. No love will ever compare. It's a level of security, knowing someone has got your back, pushing you and guiding you to where you need to be. It's a warmth in your heart when things go wrong. God is with you and will not leave you. He will comfort you.

A relationship with God, however, can also be one of the hardest relationships. You may feel like you're crying out to a brick wall sometimes. It can be confusing, not knowing what he has in store for you, wondering if your big promotion is one you should accept, whether your money troubles will ever fade, knowing where to go in life and if the path you're on, is really what God has planned for you. A relationship with God involves a lot of patience, but incredible amounts of faith. Faith in knowing he is guiding you, holding you, and working on such magical moments in your life that are going to come. You have to pray, hang in there, and trust his process.

It's all so easily said than done though. Trusting his process and his timing. You really have to let go of everything in your life and hand it all over to him. This is what I'm still trying to do in my life right now.

I'm 25 and still find it hard to let go of situations. That's me being impatient and controlling. However, if I look back at some of the stressful points in my life, and times when I've not known what more I can do, He was there. He was always there guiding me, and it all made sense later on. The fact that you can't just ring God up, have a chat and have the answers you need there and then, is hard. We are all so used to getting what we want in this day and age, so this is a difficult thing to do. Letting go and giving it all over to him.

I've been hurt by God. I've been angry with him. I've screamed in my pillow over situations which have destroyed me, leaving me wondering why God could let me feel such pain. We will all go through that with Him. The thing is, we think God is bad when he is changing us for good. Someday you will realize why that happened to you. I have on a few situations. Doesn't mean you forget about the way your heart was shattered to a million pieces, or the way you broke down countless nights in bed, waking up feeling drained of emotions. Sometimes we go through this, to get closer to Him. He did it so we would eventually come back to Him because we lost our way in the relationship. It's tough loving, but it builds us as a person, makes us realize what we want in life, and really, who will help us get that? God. It always will be.

I have grown up with the most loving parents anyone could wish for. They have always wanted the best for me in life. I've been in and out with God, but my mum and dad have never given up on me and my faith. My mum has gone through bible verses when she knew I was going through a hard time. They pray for me an awful lot, and I am ever so grateful for that. I have been so blessed in my life, taking everything into consideration. They will never give up on me and my faith with God, and I couldn't love them any more than I already do.

Everyone faces different battles during life. If you think you've got it rough, someone got it much worse than you. You can't force anyone to have a relationship with God, nor does God force every single person on the earth to have one with Him. It's up to us to enter in and build the relationship with him. There are many questions in life, as to why certain things happen. But going through life with God by your side, should never be a question. It's a whirlwind adventure and one that will blow your mind over and over again. He works in mysterious ways, but ways which will result in everlasting love in our hearts, and a life which just makes sense.

Have faith in him, walk with him, pour out your heart to him, and you'll see how your life can be completely transformed with a miracle love you never knew you needed.

9

MY BOOK OF FAITH

Jennifer Gellock

The biggest message I would like my readers to take from these written words from my soul is - the practice of unconditional love. No matter the religion you identify with, you can always pour yourself into those who differ from you because of our binding connection that is humanity. It is my hope that some of your experiences move you to become closer to your own faith while at the same time, motivate you to always have an open heart as you extend grace to those who differ from you.

One of the greatest life lessons I have chosen to deeply understand is how religion and faith are not one in the same. Religion is our identity, and it guides us on our path to experience the Divine. There are so many different world religions in the world, but all have the same goal - which is the practice of faith.

Faith to me, is a conscious choice to move closer every day to the energy that creates worlds. So, it has always confused me why world wars and hate have stemmed from religious pursuits and identities. How can some of us be "right" and while others be "wrong" in communicating with Source Energy? That's when I began to completely detach myself from the confining constructs of any one religion in order to experience the unconditional love of God. That's when I remember becoming a spiritual seeker and this is my story.

Recently, in April of 2020 during the middle of the global pandemic, I found myself lying emotionally and physically exhausted, face-up, in a yoga corpse pose on my concrete outdoor patio. World news, social isolation, and fear had officially taken its toll on me. I was searching for any relief the universe would extend my way. I remember feeling all of the weight of the world suppressing me into the ground and beginning to suck me underneath the surface. I remember wondering,

"What would happen if I just laid here and let my body become one with the Earth?"

I grew up attending a First United Methodist Church weekly in Western Massachusetts. And ironically today, I find myself living flat in the middle of the Christian Bible Belt of the United States. Ironic only because I never truly felt connected to Church and the Message within the walls of that beautiful stained-glass building. I grew to love Jesus and the symbol he represents but back then, I always left feeling a little "blah" and skeptical that a piece of the story was missing. There were bigger questions bubbling-up inside my mind that I felt no one inside those walls could ever answer. I have a brain like an academic scientist, and it has always been searching for the how's and why's of the God in the Christian Bible is who we say he is. And all of these curiosities helped me carve my own spiritual foundation rather than the rules and norms that formal religions can often oppose upon us without us ever questioning how or why we believe what we believe.

Many times after leaving my hometown and weekly church visits, I lost and found God's grace many times over throughout my 20s. God's Grace. You know, that feeling of bliss? Complete contentment? It can only be described as one of the most surreal life experiences that can't be explained but only felt deep within your own bones and spirit that tells us that "something" must be out there. It's the feeling of knowing something must be watching over you. I still couldn't figure it out but consciously chose to continue to search for answers and alignment with what was guiding me forward. I searched and I searched, and I searched for life's meaning and who God is. And eventually, I gave up the struggle of seeking and wondering and labeled myself as an agnostic in the winter of 2019 and that is when God came thundering back into my life that next spring.

Which brings me back to April of 2020. I think I laid there five days straight feeling numb, lost and searching for some meaning "out there". What else was there to do in that quarantine? It felt like all of the weight of the Universe and all of humanities' stress, historical trauma, social injustices, greed, power, and ego - laid brick by brick - like stacks on top of me, as I laid in that Alabama heat. The times were tumultuous and on the heels of one of the biggest racial justice uprisings the country had ever seen. I could feel it before it ever began. How did we get to this place? More importantly, how did I get to this place?

It was during that period of laying, asking, and releasing, that I have a very vivid memory where I consciously surrendered all of my burden to an unknown force of energy. It was like a weight had been lifted off my chest and my spirit began to float above my physical body. I would call it having been in a meditative lucid state. This, however, was not a new experience for me. I have come one with the Divine quite a few times before in my life. However, I'm not consistently great at getting back there often. But this time was different. It left me with a beacon of hope I was becoming healed and headed towards an unconditional fulfilling love that wouldn't come and go anymore. It was here to stay, and it would be everlasting.

The real answer came forward straight into my existence and washed over my physical body. I now know when you "ask" you will "receive"

So today, I sit here and can confidently say I have finally given up the struggle to fully comprehend the powerful forces of energy that I have always absorbed like a sponge as a highly sensitive and emotional person. I just know it's there. This energy most would call some sort of God. I observe this energy and appreciate it with every cell of my being. I have begun to consciously relax into the forces rather than repelling them. I choose to trust in being shaped and led forward by it rather than become suppressed by it. The swirling of energy that surrounds me, which has always been so hard for me to grasp and to relax into. But it has also always been my driving force in becoming a spiritual being. And today, I jump into the energy swirl and try to ride the waves with ease rather than get caught-up and smashed into the sand by them.

And that is my faith.

I also choose not to place my Energy Source in a box filled with labels. On any given communication and prayer, I choose to call this energy that is "Fear", "God", "Source", "Creator", "Her", "Them", and whatever name you can think of for a higher power. They are all correct in "My book of faith." Now looking back on my spiritual path and finding my faith, I can see how I relinquished all societal norms that told me this Energy must have a label of Christianity: "Jesus", "Him" or "God". I learned for myself that there is no "right" one religion because faith is our love for Source and there is no one right path to being an eternal being and experiencing God's love. They are all the right path.

Lastly, one of the most powerful spiritual lessons I have learned in this journey is to let go of the energy that fears. To lift it up off our chests and deliver it to the universe to handle. It has led me to experience more peace, joy, and harmony within me.

MEET THE AUTHORS

J. D Maxwell

JD Maxwell is from the Philadelphia area. He started writing poetry a few years back, focusing on emotional situations but has moved on to expanding his work to observational, historical, inspirational, and sometimes even comical.

Sulagna Samanta

Sulagna Samanta has currently completed her graduation. Born and brought up in West Bengal. She is scribbling down her thoughts since the age of sixteen. She finds tranquillity in articulating herself in the form of poetry, snippets, musings, micro tales and sometimes during daydreaming. She has recently tried spoken word poetry and loved every aspect of it.

Sistla Shravya

An eleventh standard amateur poet, with invisible wings. Her speaking is inversely proportional to her writings. She is fond of making some undefined feelings alive through poetry. An avid reader, aspiring student with an artistic mind.

W.P.T Moreno

W.P.T. Moreno is a German up-and-coming author of free verse poems. His work reflects on the struggles of modern life, relationships and feeling. In his world view he believes that strength can be found in ourselves as we deal with obstacles every day and still manage to make each other better.

Jagruthi Kommuri

K. Jagruthi is an E-commerce graduate, and a writer by chance who loves to write to ignite a little hope and faith in the reader. She's a simple girl who finds solace in words and writes to spread love & positivity to the world. She believes kindness goes a long way when communicated through heart.

Isidora Radovanac

Isidora Radovanac is an excellent student at Medical High School "7. April" in Novi Sad. She won fourth place at the national competition in Serbian language and many awards for thematic essays. Isidora is capable of drawing beautiful portraits and writing creative and unique tales. She's currently writing a book whose plot's related to the actual epidemic of COVID-19.

Bhavya Jain

Bhavya Jain, is a fifteen-year-old who is set on a voyage to heaven and lost his path midway and forgot the way back and uses coffee as his escape. He wants to explore more through Science and Physics and Constellations are his Best Friends.

Sam Julio Fortes Neves

Poethics is a Rotterdam based artist. With Cape-verdian roots lending himself as a writer for poetry, short stories, spoken word, podcasts and voice-overs. Boundless creativity in expression encapsulates Poethics' drive force, for the creation of his art. Poethics writes about anything with educational purpose: Religion, ethics, educational reformation, different facets of science, economics, emotional introspection, racial- and social injustice, philosophy and more.

Dr. Apteena Johnson Kakkadu

She is a twenty-three-year-old dentist as well as an aspiring writer. She has started her writing career with her debut book Lord of the words vol-1. She always loved to scribble down notes about her feelings and perspectives. She strongly believes that her writings would reflect and influence people's hearts and minds. Her writings are mostly based on women empowerment which is encouraging as well as strengthening. She also believes that healing is the utmost strength and moving on as a new being is the superior power of soul.

Kaitlyn Leiva

Kaitlyn is a full-time student pursuing her A.S. in Medical Assisting, dreaming to become a pathologist. Her drive to always learn also fuels her drive to write. Writing forces, her to learn, which in turn satiates that desire. Starting at 8 years old, 13 years later she still writes to learn, to evolve, and keep the fire burning.

Divyansh Dwivedi

He is a student and pursuing his honours in law. Besides being an athlete, he made writing his hobby. He also works with a social organisation. He was born and brought up in Kanpur, Uttar Pradesh, India. He is currently studying and residing in Noida. He also wishes to be a successful philanthropist someday.

Sarah Kesteven

Sarah Kesteven is a poet from the North of England. She studied at Kings College London and now writes poetry ranging from small longing poems to spoken word. She writes under the name

little_thoughts_at_night and is working on her debut anthology. She's a strong feminist, anti-capitalist and anti-racist and doesn't shy from speaking out against injustice, with honest and brutal words she speaks of issues from the heart and of the world and does it without fear.

Madiha Shamsi

Madiha is a person with confident personality. She is a novice to the world of expressible thoughts. Currently, she is in 11th standard. She is a beginner in the ladder of imagination. She believes that writing can heal every heart. She states that whatever happens, happens for good fortune, and she wants the same to convey the readers through her belief.

Expressing is just her way of being mentally independent.

Stuart Tucker

Stuart Tucker is a British writer and singer. Born in a rural setting and now living in London, his work often touches on the interplay between the pastoral and urban. When not writing, he can be found teaching voice or completing his mission of seeing every London street by foot.

Diksha Raman

She is basically a student pursuing her bachelor's in English honours. She is broad-minded and always prefers listening to others and gaining knowledge. She belongs to a small town called Udalguri from Assam, India. She has a deep interest towards literature and words have great impact on her as she states. The given poem portrays how spiritually she feels connected to almighty.

Rebecca Nelson

A young writer with an inclination to add many details to her writing, RJ Nelson likes to take note of others' feelings, and put those emotions on paper. In the future, she dreams of becoming a teacher for deaf children. In addition to writing poetry and music, RJ loves percussion, drawing cartoons, and seeing people smile.

Rachith Reddy

Rachith is a travel enthusiast with deep love for adventure and has a knack for storytelling. His work is roped tightly to his personal experiences, the perfectly knit and the bitter fibres alike. He brags indefinitely of his epicurean indulgences and has a true love for sports, tennis in particular. His ideology on spiritualism is atypical and far from absolute but firm, nonetheless. He is a doctor in the making and hopes to become a great surgeon very soon.

Sheryl Lazer

Sheryl Lazer, 18, is an ambitious scribbler, presently on a road to self-discovery. She believes in the power of thoughts and often makes an escape into her own world of enormous possibilities. For her, poetry transfigured from an introvert's attempt at socializing to a spiritual reconnection.

Rosanna Purkiss

Rosanna is also known as Roz. She is an open book kinda soul, wanting to explore the world, learn and connect with all kinds of people throughout her journey in life. She loves all things creative, red wine, sunshine, and the Cornish coast. Currently living in the big city of London and soaking in all the adventure!

Manoj Vaz

They say, everybody, dreams in black and white. Manoj is an award-winning copywriter with 3 decades of experience handling over 50 blue-chip clients. He has published four books: Tinsel - a hard look at Mumbai's Show Biz, The Kidnapping, and the Meth Mystery - both part of the Magic Chest Series for teenagers and Random Musings - a collection of original quotes.

Shomama Islam

Shomama is a girl who loves to write poetry. She defines herself as a girl who expresses her feelings through poetry. She is a daydreamer and a traveller. She loves to eat and overthink. Poetry is where she finds peace. She loves to write poetries about self-love and positivity.

Morgan Makowski

Morgan Makowski is new to the professional field of writing but has maintained a love for literature for many years. Her first amateur publishing was in high school and since then, she has used writing, journalism, and poetry as a creative outlet. Her inspiration comes from her faith, struggles, and life experiences. So far, she has a culmination of short excerpts and poems under her belt and is in pursuit of turning them into a published collection.

Abul Hasan Ali

As a 20-year-old with his own set of inspirations above and beyond his social obligations, Abul Hasan Ali has seen colours in dunes and forests alike, and tasted flavours beyond zest and spice. Not to undermine either of the societies he has lived as a part of, one only gains a headache in choosing between the two. Hailing from the city of Gaya in Bihar, he now pursues medicine by mornings and a fine slice of art by evenings.

Duni Porter

Duni Porter is currently a High School English teacher. She started writing when she was younger by keeping journals and diaries, but it wasn't until college that she found her voice. Writing has healed many parts of herself without even letting her know. Currently, she is pursuing her master's in counselling. She hopes to continue writing pieces while becoming continuously aware of herself and others.

Aditya Mandhania

He is a student from Maharashtra, India. He is 18 and a keen poet who loves to write to escape from this world and find peace. He also writes to raise a voice against the wrong.

Shivani Sharma

Shivani Sharma is from Agra (city of love), exactly the same person that her poetry reflects. Viz multitalented, over thinker, quirky, sensitive, versatile, soft, and romantic. She wants to try to reach the spirit with her appealing writing. She wants to serve nation and has a passion for learning something new. She's an optimistic girl, full of desires and as a co -author she has been published in one anthology. She wants to spread positivity from the heart and do social work.

Matthew Gibney

Matthew is 17 and a writer from Dublin, Ireland. He uses writing as a way to delve into his mind and as a way to stay present in the moment, which is something he has come to appreciate more as he develops his poetry, and is something he thinks a lot of people could benefit from in the bustle of modern life. When he's not writing or drinking too much coffee, he loves cross country running, going to the gym, and playing music.

Insanely Nerd

From the serene grounds of West Bengal just another nerd trying to understand the complexity of this world and people in it. Sometimes expressing her insights and lessons via mediums of poetry. Handling the situations with a lot of tolerance and a bit of kindness.

Joshua Prince

 He is a 23-year-old, mechanical engineer. From childhood he used to make up terrible stories where the characters would be his own friends. Eventually, he started scribbling down his concepts, a ballad, or his strong clingy emotions whenever he gets time. Otherwise he would busy himself trying out his own recipes or on bingeing his mom's baked goods.

Myra Lake

Myra Lake makes her home in the fringes of the Appalachian region of North America. She enjoys the quiet rural lifestyle and has a passion for expressing her thoughts and feelings through the written word. With this, she hopes to heal from and rejoice in her life experiences and inspire others to do the same.

Ranjit. K

Rêveur, a part time writer and a full-time dreamer, unravels the mysteries of life through his poems; depression and anxiety are his regular guests to be featured in his poems in one way or another. As an obscure lucid dreamer, he improvises to provide a journey through his poems in near future.

Jennifer Gellock

Jennifer Gellock is a trained academic writer by day and spiritual writer by night. She found her creative passion in the summer of 2020. In this writing piece, she tells her story of how she found herself that summer and her hopes to continue to inspire others to grow more, live more, and become more of their authentic selves through spiritual growth and acknowledgment.

OUR STORY

We're all on a Journey, and our "Writers" have made it Beautiful.

A dreamcatcher is an object made with feathers and strings, essentially used as lucky charms in many parts of the world. The same way, Inkfeathers brings together writers, editors, and artists together to form a dreamcatcher that works in favour for the young writers and readers and if you're positive about it, it may bring you luck as well.

We at Inkfeathers are connected to thousands of writers globally, who believe in the magic of telling stories. This stream of connectivity with the writers, the fact that everyone has a unique detail or edge to their story makes Inkfeathers proud to partner with these young literary as well as collaborative minds.

Back in 2013, our founders came together to form an offline group for their love of literature, and this formed collaborative energy with many young literature-wounded minds which eventually led these offline meetings to stand-ups, storytelling events, poetry slams, meet-ups to share experiences and many others. In 2016, Inkfeathers finally launched as the brand project under one Private Limited Company. This expanded opportunity gave a number of possibilities and a new way to expand our support for writers.

This dream of wanting to bring together writers as well as readers has come true beyond measure as writers connect to us from countries like United States, United Kingdom, Canada each day to bring their stories to life.

As of this year, we are extremely delighted to provide you our website (www.inkfeathers.com) where all your queries can be resolved about our self-publishing process and latest anthologies. You can get hold of the latest updates on anthologies, events, offers, new book releases and so much more here. You can go ahead and order a book from our bookstore to get a taste of our mindful curation of stories and poems.

Inkfeathers Publishing family encourages you to really put your feelings out there in words for the world to see, in order to have a common ground to grow mutually. We are a creative platform for all those seeking literary help in terms of having their words published.

Believe us, publishing a book is not easy, but we come to a writer's rescue at each phase of having their book in print in terms of Editing, Designing, Branding, Marketing and all the other work that goes behind until you have a printed copy in your hands for Distribution. Together, it couldn't have been any easier. We will be there for you, to help you turn your manuscript into a freshly bound book that sells off the glass bookshelves.

With Love,
Inkfeathers Publishing

OTHER PUBLISHED BOOKS

Hope and Beyond brings some stories of warriors; some real, some fictional who fought an unseen battle, not with a living monster but with something more powerful, our own mind and body. This book wants to test that power of sharing and test the strength in the stories of acknowledging the heavy and hazy days.

Scan the QR Code To know more & order your copy.

Taking you on some unplanned, mystical journeys into this realm of 23 beautifully mysterious minds. Little Occult Affairs has everything it takes to keep you flipping through pages trying to envisage each writer's mind and experience life, death, secrets, darkness and so much more as you dive deep in it, making you feel like you live the story itself.

Scan the QR Code To know more & order your copy.

This book will open your mind towards the untravelled purpose, the undetected significance and the unexplored value which lies within us and around us. LET THE HEART LEAD has everything it takes to make you acknowledge the spirituality that resides in all of our hearts. From "Self Ishq" to "Spirituality", from Spirit Animals to Resonance and from soul mates to twin flames, this book has it all.

Scan the QR Code
To know more & order your
copy.

Do you feel stuck in your own life? Are you going through the same motions and call it living? Have you lost your joy and desperately crave for much-needed seclusion from everything around? Behest by the malaise of hustle and chaos of big cities, Midnight Writers offers you peace in solitude, a beautiful way to embrace silence. This anthology of poems has familiar and unfamiliar terms and phrases, some modern, some long, and others freshly minted.

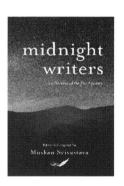

Scan the QR Code
To know more & order your
copy.

Wouldn't we love it if life were just fun and frolic? Unfortunately, life isn't idealistic. For some, it might be just a living hell. We all are here to play certain roles, but some turn out to be players. What might appear on the outside may not be entirely true. Their facade is so realistic that we can't see through and there are stories we wish weren't true. This book contains 19 such stories which belong to different genres like supernatural, contemporary fiction, horror, romance, thriller, sci-fi to suit everyone's taste.

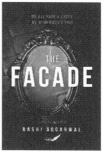

**Scan the QR Code
To know more & order your
copy.**

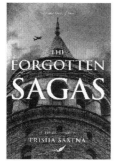

Ready to embark on a journey? From the fields of historic wars to tales of fantastic warriors. The common man stuck in the play of cosmos. The love so well cherished by the people of the past. The new light that shines as the dust over our mythology and history blows away. Are you ready to see the new light yet? The Forgotten Sagas is the ticket to this journey of yours. Through a mixture of poems and stories, it transports you not only to different parts of the world but also to the different eras seen by the human race.

**Scan the QR Code
To know more & order your
copy.**

This book is a collection of verses from around the globe, and all of the verses have their own identity which is strangely not limited to the authors writing them. Some verses are so relatable that you may be compelled to think that the author wrote those after seeing you in a similar situation, and that is not even scratching the surface of the contents of this book. Every page will take you on a journey, and every journey will seem like an adventure!

Scan the QR Code
To know more & order your
copy.

Reyansh tries to hold on to his carpet of hope for Lini as her husband silently waits for her to accept him as her true love, whereas Laxmi thinks that Evyavan is her one and only. But Evyavan has his heart swayed by someone else, and it's not Laxmi. Jay is not ready to leave Naina after a horrifying incident changed their lives forever. But then she meets her ex-flame Ranbir and old memories flood back to them. A landlady falls for

her tenant and she's determined to tear her relationship apart. As Tina tries to move on in her life with Blake, she meets Jai at a bookstore and finds her life tangled up in knots again. And these are a few of the many characters who will go through a rollercoaster ride of emotions. As they try to grapple with finding love and losing it too, one thing is for sure that their stories will keep its readers entertained.

Scan the QR Code
To know more & order your
copy.

INKFEATHERS PUBLISHING

India's Most Author Friendly Publishing House

Stay updated about latest anthologies, events, exclusive offers, contests, product giveaways and other things that we do to support authors.

 Inkfeathers Publishing

 @InkfeathersPublishing

 @_Inkfeathers

 @Inkfeathers

 Inkfeathers.com

We'd love to connect with you!

Printed in Great Britain
by Amazon